THE BLUE MOUNTAINS OF KABUTA

Hilary Wilde

CHIVERS

British Library Cataloguing in Publication Data available

This Large Print edition published by AudioGO Ltd, Bath, 2011.
Published by arrangement with the Author's Estate.

U.K. Hardcover ISBN 978 1 408 49363 2
U.K. Softcover ISBN 978 1 408 49364 9

Printed and bound in Great Britain by
CPI Antony Rowe, Chippenham and Eastbourne

cn

BLUE MOUNTAINS
OF KABUTA

7/

a

/s

Ple

You

by

or

CHAPTER ONE

Jon Hampton stood on the verandah, staring silently at the view before her. She still could not believe that it was true—this wide beautiful lawn, the trees with their crimson flowers and the purple climbers; there was even a bush covered with gardenias, their sweet fragrance drifting on the hot air while, straight ahead of her, were the mountains. Never in her life had she seen so much beauty.

'Well,' a deep voice interrupted her thoughts, 'what do you think of your inheritance?'

Jon sighed. 'I can't believe it. That anything so lovely could be mine.'

The tall man by her side chuckled. 'Don't get ideas in your head. Those mountains aren't yours.'

Jon felt her cheeks burning. 'Of course they're not, I know that, but the view is mine.' She turned to look at him, annoyed by his amused smile.

At that moment, her mother joined them, her voice tired and a little irritable. Not that she could help it, poor darling, Jon was thinking, for her mother hadn't been at all well on the plane.

'It's not too bad, Jon, but it's so terribly isolated.'

'Do sit down, Mrs Hampton,' the man, Alex Roe, said. 'I've told Dorcas to bring us out some cold drinks, or would you prefer coffee?'

Ursula Hampton smiled. 'How thoughtful of you! A cold drink, please. It was very good of you, Mr Roe, to meet us at the airport and be so helpful. I honestly don't know what we would have done without you. Don't you agree, Jon?'

Mrs Hampton glanced at her daughter, but Jon had turned and was staring again, as if hypnotised, at the scene before her.

'My pleasure,' Alex said with a smile. 'After all, Ned was my best friend.'

'But old enough to be your father.'

'Yes. Actually he was the father I needed when I took over the farm. My parents had run it and when they died and I knew nothing, Ned taught me everything about farming.'

Jon turned. She was tall, slim, with short dark curly hair clinging tightly to her head. She was not pretty and yet her face always attracted attention, perhaps because it was so contradictory. Her deep-set, dark, dreamy eyes were so unlike her small square chin. Her mouth was firm, and this, when she was thoughtful, made her look older and more mature, but for most of the time she looked about seventeen, although she was twenty-three.

She said nothing, for she felt dazed, almost as if she had been hit by a hammer and was slowly regaining consciousness. She had felt like this ever since the news came that Uncle Ned had left her his farm in Africa, plus sufficient money to run it without financial difficulty. She could not believe it. Even today, standing here and knowing it must be true, it still seemed like a dream.

Dear Uncle Ned, whom she had known for so short a time. Uncle Ned, who had comforted her so when her grandfather had died. Uncle Ned who had written to her and whose letters she had so rarely answered. Not because she didn't want to but . . .

'Jon . . .'

Her mother's voice finally pierced Jon's faraway thoughts and she turned round quickly.

'Jon, I'm just going to have a wash. Do come out of your dreams and talk to Mr Roe. You're not being very polite, dear.'

Jon smiled, 'Sorry, Mum.'

She looked up at the big man who was standing now as her mother rose and hurried inside, not—as Jon well knew—to 'wash' but to hurriedly clean her face and put on fresh make-up, for the long flight out from England must have left her feeling like a wreck. Poor Mum, Jon thought with a tenderness she would never lose, it meant so much to her to look nice.

Now, her mother gone, Jon found herself alone with this man to whom they owed so much and on whom they were dependent, not financially but for advice.

She stared at him, seeing him, perhaps, properly for the first time. A tall ugly man who yet managed to be good-looking. A square face, deeply tanned by the sun, his eyes were half-closed as he stared at her thoughtfully.

'Well?' he said. 'D'you think we might sit down and relax?'

Again her cheeks burned. 'Of course.' Hastily she sat down, tugging at her skirts. How awkward they could be, she thought irritably, still uncomfortably conscious of his amused, almost assessing look. 'Did you—did you really think I was going to be a boy?' she asked abruptly.

He smiled, and it startled her, for she saw his eyes were green. He was the first man she had ever known with green eyes. But his hair wasn't red. It was blond, almost bleached white by the sun.

She could not forget the moment when their plane landed with a slight bump and her mother, unused to flying, had grabbed her hand tightly, her lovely face frightened. They had gone down the steps and this big man had come up to greet them. It was a small airport and there was no need to produce passports and visas as they had had to do at an earlier landing.

'Mrs Hampton,' the man had said, smiling but totally ignoring Jon. 'Welcome.' Then he had looked round. 'But where is your son?'

'My son?' Jon's mother, still a little unsteady on her feet, had looked dazed. 'I haven't got a son. This is my daughter, Jon.'

And then Alex Roe had stared at her, his eyes half-closed, his mouth obviously trying not to break into a smile as he apologized.

'I am sorry. I thought Jon was a masculine name.'

Jon had blushed, thinking of how many times she had been teased about her name. Her mother had merely laughed and the matter was forgotten, but not by Jon.

Now, sitting alone with Alex Roe, Jon leant forward. 'Surely Uncle Ned told you I was a girl?'

'He always talked about his little Jon—or his heir. Never his heiress. He talked of you a lot. He loved you dearly, you know?'

Jon's eyes stung and it took her a moment to answer. 'I loved him, too.'

Her eyes grew dreamy as she kicked off her shoes and tucked her feet under her, clasping her hands. Her pale yellow frock was crumpled, the heat had caused her make-up to run, she knew her nose must be shining, her hair limp, but none of these things really worried Jon, and certainly not at a moment like this when she was looking back down the years. Nine whole years, in fact.

'You see . . .' she said, thinking aloud, not noticing the way Alex was watching her intently, 'Dad died when I was five and we went to live with my grandparents. Mum was wonderful. She had married straight from school, but now she went out to work and Gran so-say looked after me, but it was really my grandfather who did. He was known as old John, and somehow, as I grew up I hated my real name.'

'What is your real name?'

'Joanne Undine Rebecca,' Jon said solemnly, and as he laughed, her face relaxed into laughter, too. 'Now you do see why I hated it? It was too ghastly for words.'

'But why Jon and not Joanne?'

'Because everyone said I looked just like my grandfather. Same colour eyes and hair, same stubbornness.' She smiled suddenly. 'I know I am. I can be very difficult sometimes. So he was old Jon and I was young Jon ...'

She paused, no longer amused, for she saw he was still laughing, this time at her and not with her. Her cheeks hot, she looked at him.

'I don't see that it's so strange. After all, lots of girls today are called Jon. In any case, your name is a girl's. Alex is short for Alexandra.'

He laughed outright. 'That was a good try, but not a success, my little Jon. Alex is short for Alexander. Remember your history? Alexander the Great? My mother had great ambitions for me. Anyhow, please go on. You lived with your grandparents and your mother went out to work. What did you do? Learn

6

shorthand and typing?'

She hated him for the patronage in his voice. 'I went to college and am a pharmacist,' she said proudly. She had worked hard, got a good job with a high salary, her own car with money enough for regular trips to the Continent.

'A pharmacist?' He sounded more surprised than impressed. 'Well, I never did! I thought all pharmacists were men.'

'You seem to have a complex about women,' Jon said sharply. 'Do you think we're all dumb blondes?'

'You're hardly a blonde, unless you've dyed your hair,' he said, laughing, and although it was against her will, she found herself laughing as well.

'Let's return to your Uncle Ned. I gather he was the black sheep of the family?'

'Yes, but that wasn't fair. Granddad always said so. You see my grandfather had a family business. They were all architects and Ned, as the eldest son, was expected to carry on the family tradition. But he broke away and went to an agricultural college. His father understood, but his mother never forgave him. Gran was hard, at times. Nor did my mother because, you see, my father took Uncle Ned's place and . . . well, he actually died when doing a job which Uncle Ned should have been doing, surveying some land which gave way and he was . . . well . . .'

Jon paused, looking anxiously at the door that led to the house, for it was a subject her mother refused to discuss.

'Anyhow, Uncle Ned had left years before and they heard little about him, but the family solicitor had his address and when my grandparents died, Gran first and Granddad only three months later, Mr Williams, our solicitor, must have cabled Uncle Ned, because he flew back at once and took over. I don't know how we'd have managed without him.'

'And your mother? She forgave him?'

Jon sighed. 'I'm afraid she couldn't. She loved Dad so much, you see. She married him when she was seventeen and I was born when she was only eighteen, then she lost Dad when she was twenty-three, and I guess it was pretty tough.'

'But how could it have been your uncle's fault? Maybe if he'd been doing the surveying he'd have recognized the crack in the ground. Surely your mother could see that?'

Jon stiffened. 'It's easy to talk, but unless you've lost someone who means everything to you, you can't understand,' she began indignantly, but he ignored her words and went on:

'So your uncle flew over and took charge of everything. Was there much to do?'

Sighing, Jon ran her hand through her damp hair. Gosh, was it hot, she thought as she

8

found herself longing for a nice long cool bath and a drink full of ice.

'I honestly don't know. I was only fourteen, but Mr Williams had warned us that by the time the death duties were paid, there wouldn't be much money. However, fortunately he was wrong, because in the end, we had quite a nice income.'

Alex Roe smiled, took out a silver cigarette case and offered her a cigarette. When she shook her head, he nodded.

'Wise girl! Awful waste of money,' he said, lighting one for himself, then he looked at her and said casually, 'Your uncle gave you that income.'

'Uncle Ned?' Jon leant forward. 'Uncle Ned . . .?' She caught her breath. All those years and they had not known. 'I must tell Mum.'

Alex shook his head. 'He didn't want her to know. He loved you very much.'

Jon's eyes were bright. 'I loved him, too. He was so kind, so understanding, and we both had loved Granddad so much. Mum got on well with Gran, but Granddad had meant everything to me. It was terrible to lose him and somehow Uncle Ned helped me get over it.'

'When he came back, you wrote?'

Her cheeks burned uncomfortably. 'I did, but Mum . . .'

'Didn't approve?'

'No. I . . . well, I even gave Uncle Ned the

address of one of my friends, but she brought a letter round one day when Mum was there and . . . well . . .' Jon hesitated. She didn't want to tell Alex Roe, but she could vividly remember the emotional scene, her mother's tears, bitter words, accusation of disloyalty, the repetition of the old words: 'If Ned had done his duty, Dad would be alive today, because he never wanted to be an architect. It was all your uncle's fault.' Even as it hurt Jon, she had understood, for in her mother's world there was only right or wrong, nothing in between. It seemed odd that anyone so lovely as her mother could be so narrow-minded, so full of bitterness, even of hatred, yet Jon always thought it might be due to her mother's strict upbringing by aged parents, for there had to be a reason or a cause.

'I'm beginning to understand a lot of things,' Alex said slowly. 'I only wonder your mother hasn't married again, because she's most attractive.'

Grateful for the chance to change the conversation, Jon unwound her legs, letting them swing down as she leaned forward. 'I know. That's how I feel. I want her to marry again. She's so young.'

'How old are you?'

'Twenty-three.'

'You look barely seventeen,' he teased.

'Is that a crime?' she asked coldly.

'Of course not.' He laughed again. 'That

10

makes your mother only forty-one. I wonder why she never remarried. I'm sure she must have had plenty of chances.'

'Oh, she has. There was Bill in Bexhill where we lived. I liked him and I thought . . . but then we heard about this and Mum said I couldn't come out to cope with the farm alone, so she . . . she came out.' Suddenly worried by his silence, Jon looked at him. 'She's wonderful, you know. She's sacrificed a lot for me.'

His eyes narrowed thoughtfully. 'I can believe it,' he said, but something in his voice told her he didn't.

Jon twisted her hands together, avoiding looking at him, for she was hoping he could not read the thoughts in her head. Her mother's 'sacrifices', if they had been that, had been wasted. Jon had longed to work her way round the world, but how could she leave her mother who was so dependent on her?

'Did you have a boy-friend you had to leave?' Alex sounded amused and to Jon's utter humiliation, she felt her cheeks burning again.

'Yes,' she began, about to tell him of shy Jimmy, a year younger than she was and who was a marvellous dancer but that was all.

At that moment a plumpish African girl in a blue frock and crisp white apron came out on the stoep, carrying a large brass tray with glasses, bottles of orange and lemonade, and

11

an ice bucket.

'Thanks, Violet,' Alex said, and Jon stared at the girl, who gave her a quick curious look back.

Jon knew there were two maids. The other would be Dorcas, then. It seemed odd, Jon thought, to think of her new life with servants to do all the work, garden boys and a large number of farm workers. She remembered the small two-bedroomed flat on the Bexhill front with the floor polisher, vacuum cleaner and small but adequate washing machine and spin dryer. It would be odd to have no housework to do. She wondered if they did the cooking.

'Violet's the cook,' Alex said, almost as if he was able to read Jon's thoughts. He stood up, to pour out the drinks. 'A darned good one. Your Uncle Ned was fussy about his food.'

At that moment, Jon's mother joined them. She looked cool and beautiful in a yellow kaftan with loose sleeves, her dark hair shining, her long dark lashes against her creamy skin adding to the beauty of her eyes.

'How lovely—a cold drink! There's plenty of water, if you feel like a bath. Sorry I've been so long, but I suddenly felt so wet and sticky in this dreadful heat,' she said, and sat down with her usual gracefulness.

Alex passed her glass to her. 'I've arranged a cold lunch for you about one o'clock. That'll give Jon time to have a bath. Then I suggest you both rest this afternoon and I'll be along later to show you round the place and I hope, if you're not too tired,' he smiled at Jon's mother, 'I would like you and your daughter to come to dinner tonight. First nights in strange houses are always dismal and there are a few people I'd like you to meet. That is, of course, if you're not too tired,' he repeated, looking anxiously at Jon's mother.

Ursula Hampton's eyes shone. 'We'd love it, wouldn't we, Jon?' she said, and sounded so pleased that although Jon felt more like curling up in bed for the next twenty-four hours, she had to agree with a smile.

They watched the car drive down the rutty earth track, over the cattle trap and then on to the wide earth road.

Ursula Hampton turned to her daughter with a smile. 'Maybe life here won't be so bad after all, darling. He seems quite nice, doesn't he?'

Jon yawned. 'He's all right, I suppose. I must go and bath,' she said, and went inside.

*   *   *

After Jon had had her bath, the lunch was served in a square shaped room where there was a fan bringing in the breeze. It was a pleasant but simple room with white walls and dark brown antique furniture. The table was circular, there was a Welsh dresser and a long sideboard. The curtains were yellow and there

13

were yellow grass mats on the polished brown boards.

Dorcas, a thin African girl in a yellow and white check overall with a white apron, waited on them. She moved lightly and silently, but smiled when they thanked her It was a simple but delicious meal of cold ham and salad with sliced onions, tomatoes and lettuce. Afterwards they had ice cream.

'Your Uncle Ned certainly lived well,' Jon's mother said dryly.

Jon looked up quickly, but fought back the words she wanted to say. Why shouldn't Uncle Ned live well? she asked herself silently. He had earned the money. She still could not get over the fact that it had been Uncle Ned's money they had lived on for these long nine years. She longed to tell her mother, but Alex Roe had been very definite about Uncle Ned's desire for it not to be known. Surely the knowledge would make her mother think more kindly of poor Uncle Ned? On the other hand, her mother might say it was a sign of his feeling of guilt—or even that as Uncle Ned was the eldest of the family, it was his duty . . . That was something her elderly parents had taught her.

But Jon herself knew that she would never forget it. How good of him, how thoughtful and understanding.

Dear Uncle Ned who had given her the farm and the money. That had annoyed her mother.

'He should have left it to me. You're too young, Jon,' she had said angrily.

Jon had tried to find a logical reason to remove the hurt her mother obviously felt. 'He knew you were a city girl, Mum, and that my dream has always been to live in the country.'

How startled her mother had looked! 'Has it? I never knew,' she had said, but Jon had changed the subject, for it was true, her dream had always been to live near mountains where there were wide open spaces and a lake or sea. Here—the first two parts of her dream had come true, but, so far, there was no river or lake in sight!

Now, as they ate their lunch with Dorcas moving quietly round the room, Jon's mother talked of their new home.

'It's quite nice, but I had no idea we'd be so isolated, Jon. Your uncle should have thought of that. Two women living alone.'

'I expect we'll have a night-watchman, Mum.'

'If we can trust him.' Jon's mother played with a piece of bread, gazing out of the window across the valley to the distant blue-grey mountains. 'I wonder where the town is. We didn't pass any shops or houses on the way here. I wonder if we did the right thing in coming out, Jon. Maybe we should have taken Mr Williams' advice and sold the farm.'

'But he didn't *advise* us to sell it, Mummy.

15

He merely said that if we were unhappy here we *could* sell it. Uncle Ned wanted me . . . us . . . to live here and we must give it a try.'

Her mother sighed. 'I suppose so, but somehow I can't see us settling here for good. Now, be honest, can you, Jon?'

Worriedly Jon looked at her mother. How frail and unhappy she looked! If this sort of life was really impossible for her, Jon thought, but somehow she managed to smile: 'Let's give it a chance, Mum, and if it doesn't work out, we'll think about selling it.'

Her mother smiled, lifting her hand to touch her pretty dark hair. 'All right, darling, but somehow I have a feeling that we won't be here for long.'

They had coffee outside on the mosquito-screened stoep. It was very hot and the mountains were vanishing in a haze.

'It's so terribly quiet,' Jon's mother said. 'Almost eerie. I wonder if we have any people near us. It's so lonely. Maybe we're the only people for miles and miles.'

'There must be people, Mum. Alex said he would introduce us to some this evening.' Jon stifled a sigh. Strange how different she and her mother were. Already Jon loved the quiet serenity of the silence, the isolation, the scent of the gardenias, the lovely colour of the purple creepers, the tiny lizard she had just watched scuttle over the stones and up the wall as if aware of danger, but her mother was yawning, seeing none of the beauty.

'Well, I don't know about you, darling, but I feel like a good rest.'

'You are feeling better?' Jon asked anxiously.

Her mother laughed. 'Yes, but I must confess I prefer being on *terra firma*. That last flight really scared me.'

They went into the quiet house, separating to go to their own bedrooms.

Jon liked hers. It was austere in a masculine way with a single bed against the wall. Uncle Ned must have been fond of yellow for her curtains, too, were that colour. There was a chest of drawers with a small mirror on the wall and a large cupboard. But Jon stood by the open window, shielded from the mosquitoes by a screen, as she looked almost hungrily at the mountain peaks, fast vanishing in the heat haze. She unpacked, hanging up her clothes. Thinking of the trunks and crates that were coming out by sea, she knew a moment of dismay. Had they done the right thing, she wondered, making such a decision, giving up the flat, selling the furniture and rushing out here? It had been her mother's idea, *then*, yet now . . .

'Alex Roe is coming at four o'clock,' Jon's mother said urgently, standing by Jon's bedside.

Slowly and with difficulty, Jon woke up. She yawned, stretching herself. 'I must have been tired.'

'You've only got ten minutes.' Ursula Hampton hesitated. 'Jon, I wonder what we should wear tonight? First impressions are so important.'

Jon slid out of bed and shrugged. 'We'll ask him if it's black tie.'

'Black tie?'

Jon laughed. 'That's what they call it when you have to dress up. Surely you knew?'

'My friends never dressed up, unfortunately,' Ursula Hampton said sadly. 'Bill always said it was too much bother. If they knew what it means to us! It's so much more fun. Well, darling, you'd better get going. Alex Roe is a busy man and . . .'

'I know, Mum,' Jon said patiently, and hurried to the bathroom where she had a quick shower. Then she dressed, pulling on a pink cotton frock for the time being. It was much too thick, she thought. Somehow they must find some shops so that they could buy some thin dresses, more suitable for this intense heat.

She was on the stoep as the big black car drew up. Alex got out. He was wearing khaki shorts and a matching shirt. His hair was damp as he smiled at her and opened the car door.

Out tumbled three dogs who hurtled through the air towards Jon, and Alex called sharply:

'Steady on, Rex, Sandy, Jock! Calm down!'

He grabbed at the dogs and they looked up at him, their tails wagging. 'Sorry about that, Jon,' he said. 'I should have let them out one by one. These are your dogs, incidentally.'

'Mine?' Jon stared at him, her eyes wide with delight. 'They were Uncle Ned's?'

'Yes, I've been looking after them. You like dogs?'

'And how!' Jon held out her hands invitingly and the dogs came round her, sniffing at her suspiciously at first, then finally showing their acceptance of her friendliness by licking her hands.

Alex turned to open the car door for a moment. When he came back, he held a small cat in his arms. 'This is also yours,' he said. 'Little Tim, Uncle Ned called him. It was a stray kitten he found in the market, terribly thin and covered with sores.'

'He looks all right now,' Jon said as she took the small bundle of fur in her arms.

'What on earth!'

She swung round as she heard her mother's startled voice. 'Our watchdogs, Mum. They'll look after us all right.'

Alex smiled. 'You also have a good night watchman, Mrs Hampton. You have nothing to worry about.'

'It seems so lonely after living in a flat, Mr Roe.'

'I'm sure it must. Look, couldn't you call me Alex? We don't go in for formalities here.'

19

Jon saw her mother's face brighten. 'I'm glad. My name is Ursula,' Mrs Hampton said quickly, 'Alex.'

Alex Roe gave a little bow. 'Thank you, Ursula.' He turned to Jon. 'Would you care to be shown round? That is, if you want to see it all?'

'Of course,' Jon said quickly. What a stupid question, she thought. Naturally she wanted to see her farm.

Alex had turned to her mother. 'Would you care to?' but Ursula Hampton was shaking her head as she sat down. She had put on a blue skirt and thin, matching blouse. Now the boxer, Sandy, came up to nuzzle his nose against her hand.

'Some other time, Alex, thanks. I'm still tired.'

Alex nodded. Then he led the way into the house, Jon following him. 'That,' he said over his shoulder, 'is called a stoep out here. Spelled S.T.O.E.P. Not a verandah.'

'I see.' Jon had already wandered round the house, but now Alex showed her the small office with the filing cabinet, desk and typewriter.

'Your uncle was clever at figures and he has a good African clerk who does most of the work. You'll soon grasp it. Pay day is always busy, but . . .'

'How many people will I be employing?'

'Depends on the season. Being October,

this is our spring. We're ploughing and planting like mad. It's also dependent on the weather, of course. If it rains we can't plough. Most of the work is done by piece work, but of course there are a number of regular workers, too.'

They went into the lounge that ran the width of the house, with two french windows opening on to the stoep. It was an attractive room with deep comfortable armchairs, oil paintings on the walls of sea scenes, brocaded curtains, a number of small coffee tables.

'Your uncle entertained a lot,' Alex said casually. 'He was a popular man and a bachelor, too. That always helps, so he was often invited out.'

'Are you married?' Jon asked—and then wondered what had made her ask such a silly question, for she was not the slightest bit interested.

'Not yet.' Alex gave her a quick amused look. 'So far I've managed to steer clear of that hazard.'

He led the way to the kitchen. It was clean and neat with a huge fridge with its deep freeze. There was a double sink and many cupboards.

'Why didn't Uncle Ned marry?' Jon asked, thinking this did not look like a bachelor's home.

Alex gave her a strange look as he followed her through the kitchen door and they stood

21

on the concrete paving in the hot sunshine. On one side were several white buildings and Jon could hear the sound of music coming from one of them.

'Don't you know?' Alex asked her.

Jon looked up at him. What a strangely ugly face, she thought again, and looked for the word to describe it. Craggy? He had a biggish nose and a square chin and that dark sun-tan. And those strange green eyes you rarely saw, for most of the time his eyes were half closed.

'No, I don't know,' she said.

Alex looked down at her. 'He loved your mother.'

Jon's hand flew to her mouth. 'Oh, no! Poor Uncle Ned! But when . . . He'd gone away when Mum met Daddy.'

'When your grandparents died and he went over to help you out. Your mother had been a widow for nine years, but she made it very plain that she still hated the sight of your uncle.'

'Poor Uncle Ned! How wonderful if . . .'

Alex shrugged. 'I doubt if it would have worked. It's no good forgiving if you can't forget. It wasn't to be, so . . .'

Impulsively Jon caught hold of his arm. 'If he loved her, why did he leave everything to me?'

Looking grave, Alex Roe told her, 'He was afraid that your mother, in her bitterness, might refuse to accept it and that would have

22

hurt you. He wanted you to have it because he knew you loved him.'

'I see . . .' Jon said thoughtfully, thinking of the long years Uncle Ned had lived there alone, remembering the woman he loved who could never forgive him for something that was not his fault.

'We'd better get cracking,' Alex said curtly. 'I haven't time to waste.'

'I'm ready,' she said at once, frowning because he had implied that she was wasting his time and actually he had been the one doing most of the talking.

The walk round was quick, and although Jon tried to look intelligent and as if she understood everything Alex said, most of the time she was completely lost. Never before had she seen pineapples growing, but here they were, acres and acres of them, stretching away as far as the eyes could see.

Had she been asked, she might have said she thought they grew on trees like coconuts. Someone, hearing Jon had inherited a farm of pineapples, had told her seriously that they grew in the ground like carrots!

But they didn't. They grew on plants which were about two to three feet tall. The plants had long pointed spiky leaves, and had thorns with the fruit half-hidden.

'It takes two years after planting to bear fruit,' Alex was saying curtly as he strode along rapidly, Jon almost breathless but managing to keep up with him. 'You then get fruit every year. However, after five years, you have to uproot the plants, plough the land and plant again.'

He showed her the compound where the workers lived, showed her some women picking pineapples. All the time he talked brusquely, mostly over his shoulder as she tagged breathlessly behind him, and often she was lost, but somehow didn't like to ask him to explain more slowly in case he looked upon her as 'a dumb brunette'.

The dogs had gone with them, and were leaping over the pineapples, chasing the birds that came down to tease them by swooping low and then rising up in the air as the dogs barked.

As they walked back towards the house, Alex looked down at the quiet girl by his side. 'Well, how are you going to like being a farmer?'

She drew a long deep breath. 'I think I shall love it.'

She saw the amused look on his face as he asked: 'You really think you could run this farm? You don't want to sell it?'

Startled, she stood still, looking up at him. 'What makes you think I'd want to sell it?'

'A number of reasons. You're obviously a city girl, knowing nothing about farming. You could get a good price for this farm. Good money.'

'I'm not interested in money,' she said firmly. 'Uncle Ned left me the farm and I intend to run it.'

'That's very brave of you.' She could see how his mouth twisted as if he was trying not to smile. 'Now let's see how much you've grasped.'

He immediately shot a number of questions at her. She tried her best to answer them, but knew she had dismally failed.

He laughed as if triumphant. 'You've got an awful lot to learn.'

She glared at him. It hadn't been necessary to humiliate her so.

'So had you, once. You told me Uncle Ned . . .'

Alex laughed outright. 'Touché! You win and I lose. I was lucky, because I had Uncle Ned.'

And I have you, she thought silently. You may be a help, but you're also a pain in the neck.

They walked the rest of the way in silence, Jon trying to keep calm but glancing now and then at the man by her side. He was a mass of contradictions. Sometimes easy to talk to, sometimes understanding, and, at other times so horribly unpleasant.

At his car, they stopped. 'I'll pick you up at a quarter to seven,' he said curtly.

Jon remembered something. 'Mum wondered what we should wear.'

Alex looked at her and smiled. 'Clothes, little Jon, what else?'

Jon's face burned. 'You know very well what I mean. Do we dress up?'

Alex ran his hand through his hair and looked thoughtful.

'Madeleine always does. I suppose one could say cocktail party frocks. Trouser suits are acceptable.' He smiled. 'See you later.'

She watched him drive away, then turned and walked slowly towards the house. Who was Madeleine? she wondered.

* * *

As Jon showered and dressed, she thought how totally different this new life was going to be from their life in England. She was glad the dogs had come, for already her mother sounded happier as Sandy, the friendly boxer, had adopted her and now followed her wherever she went.

'What a difference it makes,' Jon's mother had said, and a lot of Jon's anxiety was lifted as her mother continued, 'That awful quietness has gone.'

Rex, the Alsatian, seemed to have chosen Jon and she already loved his questioning eyes and the way he stood close to her, not touching her but as if telling her that he was there if she needed him. Jock, the spaniel, was something of a problem, for he ignored everyone, going

26

straight for his basket under the kitchen table, curling up and going to sleep.

Jon had wondered about how to feed the dogs, but Violet, the plump, cheerful African girl, had smiled, saying she knew.

Wondering what dress to wear, Jon looked through her wardrobe. Finally she chose a dark crimson kaftan with loose sleeves and gilt trimming. She made up carefully, then brushed her hair, thinking as she did, wondering who this Madeleine was that Alex Roe had mentioned. Was she the girl he planned to marry eventually? He had joked about it, but then, with Alex, you were never quite sure when he was serious or teasing.

She put on gold sandals with flowers on the straps. She looked out of the window. Already the night was beginning to close in. The sun was going down half-hidden by the mountains, but the sky was a mixture of pale green with streaks of red and gold. How early it got dark out here in Africa, she was thinking, as the electric light suddenly went on and she heard the rackety roar of an engine. That meant they had their own engine. She had a vague memory of Alex telling her this, but there was so much to try to remember. She wondered who switched it on and off. Did it run all night?

All questions that only Alex Roe could answer—which meant that she must swallow her pride and ask them!

She sighed now as she looked in the mirror. Alex was right. She looked ridiculously young. Tonight she felt as young and helpless as she looked! It was so easy to talk confidently, but was she going to be able to run the farm— alone? She hadn't a clue. Not a single clue. Of course there was Alex to help her as he had been helped by Uncle Ned. But how long would she take to learn it all? He had his own life to lead . . . besides, she thought, as she got into the kaftan, she hated the thought of having to be dependent on him. Or on anyone, for that matter.

'Jon!' her mother called. 'Come and zip me up, darling.'

With one last look in the mirror, Jon hurried to the next room. It was similar to hers, but the colour scheme was different. In here the curtains were made of deep red and black striped material with a matching rug.

Her mother was peering into the mirror. 'How can you be expected to see in this bad light?' she was grumbling. She was wearing a long green velvet gown. Its very simplicity ensured its elegance, Jon thought. Her mother had brushed her dark hair up, piling it high on her head. She wore a diamond necklace and matching ear-rings, but, Jon thought with dismay, wasn't it rather overdressed for a cocktail party? Knowing how sensitive her mother was, she was tempted to remark on this, but then decided to say nothing.

Sandy, the boxer, lay patiently watching as Jon did up the long back zipper.

'You look super, Mum.'

Her mother smiled. 'Thanks, darling. First impressions are so important. I wonder what sort of social life one has here. I do hope we make lots of friends. It would be so nice to have a full social life,' she added, almost wistfully.

Jon looked at her in dismay and hoped her face didn't show it. Surely her mother couldn't mean it? she thought. A farm in an isolated district hardly promised a busy 'social life'. They'd probably get to know a few families around, but . . .

'You had friends in Bexhill, Mum.'

'They were so boring, Jon. Bill never stopped talking about cricket. Sometimes I wanted to scream. When is Alex picking us up?'

'In ten minutes. I must just finish my face.'

'Let me look at you, darling. A pretty frock, but . . . well, Jon dear isn't it a little . . . well, casual? I mean a kaftan is only a housecoat, after all.'

Jon smiled, wondering what her mother would say if she pointed out that if a kaftan was 'casual' a long velvet gown had gone to the other extreme.

'Kaftans are all the rage in the fashion world, Mum. Besides, it is comfortable. See you in a moment.'

29

In her room, she stared round, surprised. In that short space of time while she had been with her mother, either Dorcas or Violet had quietly come in, turned down the bed, pulled the curtains across and tidied away the dirty clothes.

Jon laughed at herself. Now she was a lady of leisure with two maids to look after her, so she must adapt to this new life. How strange it seemed after life in Bexhill, for she had always been the tidy one, cooking the meals, doing the washing, tidying things away, for she knew her mother got very tired doing her job as hotel receptionist and book-keeper, though she never complained.

Having one last look at her reflection in the mirror, Jon asked herself a question.

'Tell me, Jon, are you going to like this new life?'

She scowled at herself, her firm young mouth tightening. She most certainly was. This was what Uncle Ned wanted. That she should have the farm and enjoy life here just as he had done.

'Jon,' her mother called, 'Alex is here.'

'Coming!'

Unconsciously she braced herself and as she joined them, seeing her mother talking eagerly to the tall man, she was prepared for that familiar look of amusement in his eyes.

'All right,' Jon said wearily. 'You don't have to tell me. I look younger than ever.'

Alex put his head back and laughed. 'You read my thoughts so accurately, but why get so mad about looking young? In twenty years' time you'll be glad you do.'

'In twenty years' time I'll . . .'

'Look twenty-three,' he teased.

'She always looked young,' Ursula said.

Alex turned to her at once. 'And so do you, Ursula. You look ridiculously young to have a daughter of twenty-three. You must have married out of the cradle.'

Jon saw the glow of happiness in her mother's eyes. Bless her, Jon thought, this was just what her mother needed. In Bexhill, they'd known so few people of her mother's age group. Most were too young or too old.

'I had just left school,' Ursula admitted as they went out to the car, a path across the dark grass shown by the lights of Alex's car.

'The dogs . . .' Jon said worriedly.

Alex laughed. 'They know. You just have to say *Stay* and they'll wait for your return.'

'I'm just not used to this way of living . . .' Jon began.

Alex was holding open the front door of the car for her mother, so Jon got in the back.

'You'll get used to it, little Jon,' he said as he slid in behind the steering wheel. The sky was fast darkening, but the car's headlights blazed a bright trail ahead as he drove slowly. 'Sorry about the bumps, but nearly all our roads are just earth tracks.'

31

Jon sat in the back quietly, listening to the two in front as they talked. Suddenly she felt nervous, wondering what sort of people they were going to meet. Would her mother find anyone who shared interests in common, who, as Uncle Ned used to say: 'talked the same language'? Would her mother find it possible to make friends here? Or would she go on being unhappy?

Jon dreaded the thought of being torn in two by her different loyalties—her love for her mother as against her strong feeling that she must carry out Uncle Ned's wishes and live on and love his farm. Jon could only hope that such an occasion might never arise or she be asked to make a decision between the two.

The car slowed down outside two big gates. Jon could see a high wire fence.

'Does . . . does our land come up this far?' she asked.

'Yes. Your land runs alongside mine,' Alex said as a tall African came to open the gates and lift his hand in greeting.

'Why the high fence?' Jon asked as they drove through and she saw the African closing the gates behind them.

'Because I haven't got a *farm*. It's a wild life sanctuary. I doubt if you'll see much tonight, but I have several giraffes, ostriches, impalas and a lot of wild birds.'

Jon leaned forward eagerly. 'What fun!

'It's also hard work,' he said dryly. He drove

up a steep climbing track and Jon saw that while her farm was in the valley, Alex's was on the side of the mountain that was behind her farm and on which none of the windows looked, suggesting that the builder of the farmhouse had preferred the distant mountains to the overpowering closeness of the one behind him.

'I thought you farmed. You said Uncle Ned . . .' Jon began.

'Yes,' Alex laughed 'I loathed pineapples, and judging from the way they behaved, I reckon they loathed me. I was not a success like your uncle. In the end, I gave up. I still grow some things, of course.'

'Such as?'

'Well, a little citrus, cotton, tomatoes, beans, potatoes, but most of my land is used for wild animals that are being slowly eliminated from our world.'

'But that can't pay!'

'Really, Jon!' her mother put in. 'It's no business of yours.'

But Alex laughed. 'Naturally she's interested now she's a Farmer. Frankly, my place doesn't pay yet, but I have other means of support. However, one day it will when I open it to visitors. We get a lot of tourists up here. Ah . . .' His voice changed because of what was before them.

Jon caught her breath with delight as she watched the little deer-like impala, caught in the bright glare of the headlights as they leapt high—some, in confusion, bumping in mid-air, caught in the light at one moment, vanishing into the dark night the next, they were like tiny ballet dancers.

'They must be rather a hazard when driving,' her mother said.

'They would be out on the main roads, but I tell my friends that they must drive slowly here. Well, Jon, what did you think of them?'

'Absolutely lovely!' Jon's voice had a dream-like quality. 'Incredibly beautiful. I've never ever seen anything like it.'

The track ahead curved and suddenly the headlights shone on the house. Surprisingly, to Jon, it was a modern house, built L-shaped with a long verandah . . no, Jon corrected herself, stoep, of course. It had huge picture windows with curtains drawn but light glowing through them.

As the car stopped, Jon noticed there were two other cars already there.

'Then we're not the first?' she asked, unaware of the dismay in her voice.

'Madeleine always comes early to get everything organized. Or,' Alex's voice was amused, 'she likes to think she gets them under control. I have a very good houseboy, Jeremiah, who doesn't need help. He's been with me for ten years.'

Alex opened the car door and helped Ursula out while Jon was scrambling

34

ungracefully from the back seat. There were large lamps on the front of the house, throwing light over the paved courtyard.

As they went up the few steps to the stoep, the door opened.

'There you are at last, Alex! I wondered . . .' an impatient feminine voice began, and then Jon saw her. It could only be Madeleine, she thought—and thought rightly.

Madeleine was tall with the sort of figure every woman wants. Slim, she looked perfect in a long white silk frock, with matching white sandals. Her blonde hair was twisted up into a high elegant style, and she wore green emerald ear-rings. Her blue eyes were wide with amazement as she stared at Alex's companions.

'Who on . . .' she began, but Alex gave her no time to finish the sentence.

'Ursula, I want you to meet Madeleine Cox. Her parents have the farm on the other side of me. Madeleine, this is Mrs Hampton and her daughter, Jon.'

'Daughter? But we thought . . .' The beautiful girl stared at Jon, her eyes assessing her, Jon felt.

Alex laughed. 'I know. Everyone thought that, but it seems that she's called Jon after her grandfather. Who has come?'

'The Joneses. Come in.' Madeleine seemed to remember her manners and turned to Ursula.

'We'd like to,' Alex said dryly, 'if you'd move out of our way.'

For a moment, Madeleine looked startled, then annoyed, and then she laughed. 'I'm sorry, I didn't realize I was blocking the way.'

The house was even more beautiful inside than out, Jon thought, as Alex led the way. The lounge went the length of the house, the long part, and was furnished with perfect taste and comfort. Somehow, though, it didn't look like a man's house, she thought, then realized that his parents had lived here before him and that the silk curtains of that lovely peach colour were more likely to be his parents' choice than his. The deep comfortable armchairs, the family portraits on the walls, the huge lamp shades and the different yet related colours made the room very beautiful.

The Joneses were a middle-aged couple, he as fat as his wife was thin. They welcomed the newcomers and soon Ursula was sitting on the couch with them, answering questions, her face bright, her eyes shining.

Gradually more and more visitors arrived until there were twelve. Jon, never one with a good memory, found it difficult to fit the name with the face, but she vaguely knew there was a Larry, a Ray, a Nina, an Annabelle, a Peter. One couple was young and obviously very much in love, another couple were in Ursula's age group and talked mostly to her. The most maddening part for Jon was that everyone expressed surprise and amusement because she was a girl and not the boy they expected, and she found herself growing more and more irritable and wishing that she had been called Jo-Anne.

Dinner was served in a round room with a round table. The satinwood furniture gleamed and was matched by the beautiful silver and glass. The curtains were a deep rose pink that matched the rugs on the polished floor.

Prawn cocktails were followed by a wine-rich consommé followed by tender tasty venison and then by fruit salad. Jeremiah, a tall African in spotlessly white shorts and jacket, served them perfectly, helped by Natalie, the African girl in a black dress with white pleated apron and a tiny white cap perched on top of her black curls. Jon and Ursula sat on either side of Alex and he turned to Jon, as if able to sense the question in her mind.

'My mother was old-fashioned and she loved to cling to the days gone by, so she insisted on Natalie's predecessors wearing this uniform. Actually Natalie deems it an honour to wear it, for she sees it as a status symbol and that it makes her far more superior than the other servants. They're like children,' Alex said with a tenderness that surprised Jon. 'I'm lucky to have them both.'

It was a pleasant evening with Alex being the perfect host, yet Jon felt out of it.

Everyone talked to her, but somehow she wanted to be left alone. There was so much to think about, so many problems to solve. At least her mother was happy, Jon thought, listening to her gay laughter.

Madeleine acted the part of the hostess, though Alex seemed to ignore her. Not that she ever let him, for she was constantly asking him for a cigarette and when he held out his lighter, her hand would steady his and she would look up at him with a special sort of smile.

Later, she came to sit by Jon.

'Quite happy?' she asked, her voice husky. 'I imagine we're all rather oldies in your eyes, because you are very young.'

Jon bit back the angry words. 'I'm twenty-three.'

'Really?' Madeleine's voice gave the impression that she didn't believe Jon for one moment. 'I'm twenty-seven and Alex is thirty-five,' she went on with a little laugh. 'Just a nice difference.'

'You're engaged?' Jon asked.

Madeleine laughed again. 'Not officially, but we have an understanding. Alex works so hard and has so much planned ahead that I don't know when we can fit in a wedding. What are you going to do? Sell the farm, of course.'

Jon stiffened. 'Why *of course*?'

'Alex is sure you will. After all, what do you

know about farming? Besides, this is no life for a girl like you. You couldn't live alone.'

'My mother is living with me.'

'For how long?' Madeleine looked at Jon with contempt in her eyes. Both girls looked across the room to where Ursula stood, talking to the young couple now, laughing, looking lovely. 'Just how old is your mother?' Madeleine asked, a strange note in her voice.

'Forty-one. She was eighteen when I was born.'

'She looks even younger,' Madeleine said thoughtfully, and then turned to Jon. 'She'll marry again, that's for sure, then you couldn't live here alone.'

The patronage in Madeleine's voice riled Jon so much that she felt she must hit back.

'Maybe I shan't be alone,' she said with a smile. 'Maybe I'll be married, too.'

CHAPTER TWO

Much later that night, Jon lay awake, trying in vain to fall asleep. It was partly due to the tiredness that had swept through her that evening and partly, she felt, because of the emotion roused in her as they talked so nicely of Uncle Ned, so affectionately, so full of praise, and then she had happened to glance at her mother and had seen the bitterness on her face, still there after nine long years. Jon could see that her mother longed to interrupt the conversation, to say that Uncle Ned was a bad man because he had not only let down his family but was the *indirect* cause of her husband's death. But would she have called it *indirect*? Jon had wanted to cry, then. If only her mother, she had thought, could overcome this senseless hatred of Uncle Ned?

However, the evening had not been altogether sad, she comforted herself, for her mother had really enjoyed herself and they had come back to their new strange home, with Jon's mother full of excitement because Alex was taking them to the club next day and they would meet even more people.

Jon had been puzzled. 'I thought you hated watching cricket?' she had said, remembering the arguments at home about watching it on TV.

'This is cricket with a difference,' her mother told her. 'They also play bowls and tennis and there's a swimming pool, so you don't have to *watch* cricket all the time. Alex will propose us as members and . . .'

'I don't think I want to join . . .' Jon had begun, but the dismay on her mother's face had made her hastily add, 'but of course I will. One must be friendly in this sort of place.'

It was dark in the bedroom as she lay there, trying to sleep. Every now and then there was a strange creak as if someone was tiptoeing along. The blackness of the night seemed to be suffocating her, moving in.

Of course, she told herself, it was stupid childish imagination. Simply because she was used to the reflection of the street lamps through their windows in their Bexhill flat it made this intense darkness seem much worse, seem almost threatening.

There was no moon and although the stars twinkled in the purple black sky, there was no light at all. Just this heavy blackness.

She could hear Rex's breathing. He was sleeping on the mat by her bed. It comforted her, for she was not completely alone. Sandy, the boxer, was sleeping under the bed of Jon's mother, but the spaniel slept alone in the kitchen.

'Jock is grieving for Uncle Ned,' Alex had explained that evening. 'He'll never be quite the same, because he's no longer young and it's hard for an old dog to accept a new master. But don't let it worry you. He'll be all right if you let him jog along and one day he'll accept you—that is, if you're here long enough!'

Now, remembering this, Jon sat up and pummelled her pillows angrily. Why did everyone take it for granted she would sell the farm?

Madeleine had given her no peace. 'A rooinek like you can't handle the staff,' she had said.

'And what is a rooinek?' Jon had asked.

41

'A pommie . . . an Englishman. It means red neck because you all burn in the sun.'

A man sitting near them had laughed. 'Look who's talking! You were a rooinek once, Madeleine.'

She had laughed, 'That's years ago, when I was a child.'

'Once a rooinek always a rooinek,' a young man with short blond hair had teased.

Jon sighed, stretched and tried to find a comfortably cool spot on the pillow. There had been another strange moment she had noticed but not understood. She had been talking to Mr Jones and he was telling her something when he jumped and gave a hastily hidden little groan. But Jon had seen why he'd made that strange noise. His wife had kicked him!

What had Mr Jones said? She closed her eyes and battled to remember. She tried to recall the conversation. What had they been talking about? Suddenly she knew.

They had been joking about her name, saying everyone had taken it for granted she was a man, and then Mr Jones had begun:

'Well, if he can't *buy* the farm, then he . . .' and it was then Mr Jones' wife kicked him.

But why? What would the rest of the sentence have been? she wondered. 'If he can't buy the farm then . . .' Then—what?

And why, she asked herself again, why was everyone so *sure* she wanted to sell the farm?

Surely when you inherit something you

don't immediately sell it? Not without giving it a trial, anyhow.

Another annoying part of the evening had been Madeleine with her patronizing air and sarcastic remarks. She had rattled off a series of questions, barely waiting for the answers.

'Did you have to work in England?'

'It must be pretty dreadful there with the sun never shining and everyone in such a mess. Hadn't you a car? How positively ghastly!' and then the way her voice had changed, become disbelieving. 'Oh, you did have a car. I wonder you could afford it.'

Then, when Madeleine had learned Jon was a pharmacist, she had told everyone.

'Just think, Uncle Ned's little Jon is a pharmacist, whatever that is!'

Everyone had laughed. Alex had joined in the teasing.

'Don't you know? She mixes medicines, counts the pills and we'd all better watch out for she must know a lot about poisons!'

While everyone laughed, Jon had—to her subsequent shame—lost her temper.

'There's much more to it than that,' she had said crossly. 'You need a degree, and it's a highly responsible and well-paid post.'

Even as she spoke, she knew she had made a mistake. She should have laughed with them instead. She had known at once how stupid she had been, for she had seen the smile Madeleine had given Alex—the sort of pitying yet exasperated smile the behaviour of a child can make you give.

'We're only teasing you, little Jon,' Alex had said and it had made everything much worse. Jon had sat still, painfully conscious of her red cheeks as Alex deftly changed the conversation.

Later he had come to sit with her, his voice reproachful.

'Your mother's very tired, Jon. It's time you went.'

And Jon had stared at him, tempted to say that she had twice suggested going home to her mother and each time her mother had frowned, saying: 'We can't go yet. It would be rude. Besides, we have no transport, so we must wait for Alex to suggest it.'

Now he had, blaming Jon for staying!

When he had driven them home, he showed Jon how to switch off the electricity.

'You can't leave it on all night, Jon. Tomorrow I'll show you it. Leonard's task is to heat the water, cut the wood, and cope with the electricity, but sometimes he forgets, so it's just as well if you know how to do it.' Alex had talked of it casually as if it would be the easiest thing in the world, but Jon felt nervous, for she had never been very bright with things mechanical and she could only expect to make a fool of herself.

Then Alex had shown her how to lock the windows and outside doors. He gave them torches to have by their beds and showed them the candles and matches in case they needed them, and finally told them to leave the bedroom doors open and let the dogs roam the house.

'That way no one can break in. Besides, there's always the night watchman.'

Then Alex had gone and suddenly the house seemed very quiet. Jon had sympathized with her mother, who openly admitted her fear.

'I don't think I can stand this, Jon.'

'If Alex says it's all right, it must be,' Jon had said. 'He wouldn't let us stay here alone if he wasn't sure.'

But now, with her mother sound asleep and the strange creaks in the air, Jon wondered. Alex could be wrong . . .

Now as she lay in the oppressive darkness, she was glad when she heard Rex scratching himself. You're being very stupid, she told herself, you're not alone and nothing can happen.

Just at that moment, the dogs leapt up and began to bark shrilly. Jon's hand groped for the torch and finally found it. The dogs were in the lounge, leaping at the window. Somehow she pulled on a dressing gown and followed them, her torch alight, throwing a bright beam ahead.

She saw the faint beam of a torch lighting the front path and shone her torch on the man she could see faintly.

The glare of the torch showed his startled face. She recognized the night watchman, as Alex had pointed him out before he left; a slightly stooping African, carrying a knobkerrie and a torch as he did his rounds.

Just how stupid could she be? Jon asked herself as she went back to bed, first looking in on her mother, who had slept peacefully through the noise, and wished, for a moment, that she had taken her mother's advice and swallowed a sleeping pill.

She lay down. This time she was going to sleep, she told herself, despite all the creaks and blackness.

When she awoke, the sun was pouring into her room. She felt something jump on her bed and cuddle up close, lying on her leg. It was the little cat. Rex chose that moment to stand up, stretching his legs, looking at Jon, then lying down again, rolling over on his back, waving his legs in the air, then jumping up to come to her side to lick her hand.

Jon looked up at the high raftered and thatched roof and at the huge timbers that held it aloft. She gently tugged at Rex's ears; he seemed to like it and a sense of happiness swept through her. This was home—her home, a home given to her by someone who had loved her very much. Surely that alone should make her happy?

She heard furniture being moved, a burst of

laughter and then Dorcas brought in a tray with a small teapot, cup and saucer, milk and sugar.

Jon yawned and smiled; it was a change from her old life. She had always gone to work earlier than her mother, so had taken a breakfast tray into her before leaving. Now, she thought, she was also being waited on. Later she bathed and dressed and the dogs— for the boxer had come from her mother's room—were jumping up excitedly. Jon saw her mother was still asleep, not having even noticed the tray of early morning tea, so she went out through the kitchen as the two girls were still polishing the floor in the lounge. Even Jock, the quiet unhappy spaniel, followed her.

Jon drew a long deep breath of the warm air and looked up at the mountain that towered above them. Up there was Alex's wild life sanctuary. There was a red earth track, rutted with the wheel marks of the tractors that drove over it daily, and the dogs had raced ahead so she followed them. Sandy and Rex were leaping across the pineapple plants, racing in circles while Jock, poor old darling, trotted along slowly just behind her and when she stopped and put out her hand, he sniffed at it and walked by. Poor Jock, how he must have loved Uncle Ned—but how could you explain to a dog what had happened to a beloved master?

Although she enjoyed the walk, glancing all the time at the beautiful distant mountains across the valley, she was sticky with heat when she got back, so she had a quick shower and changed all her clothes, for they were damp from the heat, too. There was a large linen basket in the bathroom, so she dropped them in. Just think of having all your washing done for you! She wondered if the girls understood how to wash drip-dry clothes, for all of hers were, though oddly enough, her mother preferred clothes that had been ironed. That would keep Dorcas and Violet pretty busy if this heat continued.

A little bell tinkled and Jon found that breakfast was ready—a delicious grapefruit followed by a boiled egg. Jon took her mother's in to her, for she was waking up, still sleepy and not very happy.

'Did you sleep well, Jon? It took me ages to go off and then I had an awful dream. The dogs barked like mad and a burglar . . . What? My breakfast. Yes, of course. Thank you, but I don't know if I feel like eating.'

'Just try, Mummy,' said Jon. 'Alex is coming down at nine to show me how the electricity works and then, remember, we're going on to the club.'

Her mother's face brightened. 'Of course! What a dear Alex is. Why don't you like him, Jon?'

Jon was startled. 'Why . . . why don't I like

48

him? But I do . . . well, in a way.'

'Ah, that's so typical of you, darling. You're so cautious in case you get involved. Your father was the same.' For a moment, Ursula's face clouded with grief. Then she smiled: 'Not that you could ever get involved with Alex. You're far too naïve and young. He needs a more sophisticated woman.' She chuckled. 'Madeleine is being very stupid, acting so obviously.'

'Obviously?' Jon echoed.

'Oh, Jon darling, don't be so dumb. Isn't it obvious to everyone that she intends to marry Alex?' Ursula laughed. 'She hasn't a hope. He's not a fool. You must have noticed the way she bosses him around, fusses, makes out she's the hostess—and then of all the corny habits to hold his hand as he lights her cigarette! I thought that went out in the early thirties. Oh, I know she's beautiful, but she's too brash, to my way of thinking. She thinks she has Alex like a puppet on a string.'

'You don't think she has?' Jon asked. 'She seems very sure.'

'I doubt it very much. A man like Alex dislikes being chased so obviously. I think he's a darling. Have you any idea how old he is?'

'Madeleine told me he was thirty-five.'

'Is that all? I'd have thought he was nearer forty . . .' Then Jon's mother smiled. 'Run along and eat your breakfast or your egg will be cold. What a chatterbox you are!' she added

49

affectionately.

The egg and coffee were both cold and Jon sat looking at them, strangely puzzled. She had never heard her mother speak so well of any man before. Bill had been all right, but he had his faults. So had George, the one before. But apparently to her mother, Jon thought, Alex was perfect. And that strange remark about age. Her mother had thought him nearer forty.

Jon half closed her eyes, seeing Alex's rugged suntanned face. Did he look as old as forty? Her mother was a very young forty-one, gay and attractive.

Jumping up, she went to the window. Was that why Mrs Jones had kicked her husband? Had they had the same idea that was now in Jon's head?

Was Alex being so nice to them because he planned to marry her mother?

Jon caught her breath. Mr Jones had said: 'If he can't buy the farm . . .'

But Alex didn't want to buy the farm. At least, he had never said so.

Suddenly she heard the sound of a car coming, and turned and drank the unpalatable coffee, for he might remark on it and then give her a lecture on chatting too much! She was waiting on the stoep when he arrived.

'How did things go last night?' he asked.

He was wearing what she had been told was called a safari suit—a pale grey jacket and shorts with matching knee-length stockings and dark shoes. Surprisingly elegant, she thought, staring at him.

'Fine,' she said with a stiff smile, for nothing would ever make her tell him of her fright in the night!

But it was no good. His smile showed that he knew.

'You gave old Robert a fright, shining your torch in his face like that.'

Jon's cheeks burned. 'The dogs barked. I had to investigate.'

Alex smiled. 'You're so right, little Jon. The dogs were wrong to bark, because they should have known his step, but it's not a bad idea really, for any casual prowler hearing that noise would stop and think twice about breaking in. Are you ready to see the electric plant? You think you can cope?'

She lifted her head and looked up at him, her mouth a thin line of determination.

'Of course I can cope,' she said with a confidence she didn't feel, but, as she followed him, she wondered what choice she had. Uncle Ned loved this farm and her and somehow or other, with or without Alex's help, she must be able to cope.

Alex looked over his shoulder and smiled. 'Know something, little Jon? I wouldn't be a bit surprised if you can.'

CHAPTER THREE

Alex drove them to the club about eleven o'clock. The sun was bright and the air humid, but the blue sky had huge white clouds piling up and Alex said there might be a storm later.

Ursula, sitting next to him, shivered. 'How I hate thunderstorms! They terrify me.'

He smiled. 'You'll get used to them, but they can be pretty frightening. Don't worry, you'll . . .'

'Get used to them!' Jon echoed, sympathizing with her mother who was, she knew well, really frightened of so many things. 'You're always saying we'll get used to things.'

Alex turned his head. 'Because it's the simple truth, little Jon. When you have no alternative, you have to accept conditions as they are and, in time, you get used to them.'

'I absolutely agree, Alex,' Ursula said quickly. 'One adjusts in time.'

Jon stifled a sigh. Once again she was wrong! She looked out of the window of the car. They had driven along the valley on a rutted bumpy track, but were now on the main road, if such it could be called, for though it was wide, it was an earth road with corrugations that made the car jolt and bump. The heat already was terrific. She found herself wishing that it would rain. She wanted to laugh, to tell them how fantastic it all seemed to her—this new strange life with no beds to make, no breakfast to cook, no dishes to wash, no floors to polish, no ornaments to dust—but she hesitated. Alex was sure to use anything she said as a weapon against her, making her feel small, and her mother would back him up.

She sighed again, looking at the tall trees that lined the road, the mud huts with their thatched roofs, the small children playing outside, pausing to look up as the car roared by.

After her packed days in England, her busy life, she wondered how she would fill the long empty days here, then smiled ruefully, for she had no problem. She was going to get all the books she could in order to read up about farming, particularly pineapples.

Now she half-closed her eyes, trying to remember just what Alex had told her about their electricity. At the time Alex had made it sound simple enough, pull here, press there and so on, but now, looking back, it seemed like double dutch to Jon. Perhaps it might be a good idea to go out and watch Leonard start the engine, but then she knew that was not a good idea. Leonard would tell Alex and once again Alex would have a weapon with which to bait her. She sighed. The only thing was to cross her fingers and hope Leonard would never forget to put the electricity on, for she felt sure she could never cope with the intricate-looking machine that Alex called 'simplicity itself.'

They must be getting near the village—if that was what they called it out here—for they were passing gates with painted signs containing the farm names and she could vaguely see, through the trees, white buildings, many with thatched roofs. As they passed a long building, Alex told them it was the stores and the post office; later they passed a garage. At last they reached the club, going off the main road along a curving drive lined with trees and flowering shrubs. Everywhere, Jon thought, there was colour—deep crimson, bright purple, vivid yellows of the cannas and the creamy white of frangipani. The clubhouse was an attractive long building with a wide stoep facing the cricket field where white-clad figures were standing in the blazing heat.

Jon caught a glimpse of a tennis court and also the bowling green, where the bowlers, all in white with hats on, stooped to play and then walked. How could they stand the heat? Jon wondered. Maybe in time one got used to it?

The club itself was lofty and delightfully cool, the long picture window running the whole length of the building giving a wonderful view of the mountains Jon loved so much. There were groups of chairs round small tables and a big bar at one end with open windows leading to the kitchen.

They could hear the children shrieking with delight as they jumped into the swimming pool. Most of the watchers were sitting outside on the roofed stoep. Now Alex led Jon and her mother outside and introduced them to the club members.

As usual Jon found herself asked the same questions.

'Can you run a farm?' 'Are you going to sell the farm?' 'We thought you were a man—how did you get such a funny name?'

Jon tried to smile, to laugh, to hide her irritation, but it grew until a big red-faced man with white hair smiled sympathetically and said: 'My number's in the book, so just give me a ring if you need help. Your Uncle Ned was my best friend,' and Jon knew he meant it and that perhaps she was seeing these questions in the wrong light. Maybe they were concerned for her, maybe they were worried as to what would happen to Uncle Ned's beloved farm.

When lunch was served, it was a well-organized, delectable meal. Ursula was sitting at a table of bowlers and she looked happy, so Jon went to get her own lunch and found Alex by her side.

'We'll sit out under the trees,' he said.

Jon hesitated, looking at him, suddenly aware of the small silence around them which made her feel everyone was watching them.

'All right,' she agreed, and followed him out into the hot air, holding his plate for him while

55

he got two chairs and arranged them under a tree and near a table.

As they sat down, Alex looked at her thoughtfully.

'You're hating all this, aren't you, Jon?'

The hot colour raced to her cheeks. She looked at him with dismay. 'I'm . . I'm not *hating* it, but . . .'

'Yes, you are. Now eat up or the chicken'll be cold. This kind of casserole is Mrs Kemp's speciality and she does it well. Then I'll get us some ice cream and we can talk.'

What about? she wondered unhappily, but grateful for the delay she enjoyed the delicious chicken with the mushrooms and new potatoes.

Suddenly she thought of something. 'Shouldn't I have paid for this?'

'You're my guests.'

'But, Alex . . .' she began, and hesitated. 'Thank you. Is . . . is Madeleine here?'

He looked round vaguely. 'I don't know. Sometimes she comes, but she gets bored here. You are, too, aren't you?'

'I'm not bored. I just feel . . . well, it's all so different . . .'

'From your old life. You're shocked at the easy way we live with our servants and no work to do. You're even rather shocked at the way everyone is enjoying himself here, playing in the heat, watching and gossiping, or lying in the sun. What else should they do at the

56

weekend? Have you any idea how hard a farmer works? Even if he has employed staff, he has to organize and check everything. As for the wives, they often help run the farm, handle the accounts or have children to look after. Jon, you have one big fault. You judge people, but never yourself.'

She was startled and hurt. 'That's a horrid thing to say!'

He smiled. 'But true.'

'It isn't true! I don't judge people . . .'

'Yes, you do. I watched you last night. What you must guard against, Jon, is getting smug. There's no one so unpleasant as a smug woman unless—' he chuckled, 'it be a smug man.'

'I'm not smug!' Jon could hardly speak, she was so upset. 'I don't judge people.'

'You do, you know. Nor have you much sense of humour. You see everything from a personal angle, but not from the other person's. For instance, you say you want your mother to marry. Right? But why? Not because you want her to be happy but so that you can be free.'

Jon's eyes widened with dismay as she stared at him. Was he right? She had often wanted to be free to work her way round the world. Was that the sole reason she wanted her mother to marry again—in order to be free?

'I don't blame you in the least,' Alex went on, his voice casual as if they were discussing the weather. 'Girls of your age need to break away and see the world. The last thing they want to do is to sit at home and look after Mummy—especially when Mummy is so young and attractive.'

Jon's mouth was dry, but she let him go on. He was right, in a way, though she had never realized it before. In England she had often resented her mother's dependence on her and her fussing if Jon came home late. After all, as Jon knew she had often thought, surely at twenty-three years of age, you were capable of looking after yourself?

'Another thing, why do you get so upset when you're teased?' Alex went on, putting his empty plate on the table and leaning forward.

All round them there was laughter and voices, but to Jon, it was as if she and Alex were in a small world of their own from which she wanted to escape but knew he would not let her.

'Jon,' he was saying, 'surely you must be used to being teased about your name by now, but you still get angry. Why? Your job, too. How upset you were about that. Why? We all know how important a job a pharmacist has. After all, people's lives are in your hands. We know this, so why did you get so angry? Have you an inferiority complex?'

Jon stared at him. Suddenly she knew the truth. She had an inferiority complex. But only since she met him! Yet how could she tell him that? 'I don't think so, but everything's happened so fast and . . . and I'm not used to being teased. Most of my friends know me well and . . . well . . .'

'You don't mind when they tease you.' He stood up. 'I'll get us ices. Like chocolate? Good. I won't be long.'

'Alex, what about Mum?'

He smiled. 'She's being looked after. I've seen to that, so don't worry,' he said, and walked away.

She sat very still, looking at her hands. Was he right? Was she quick to judge others? Perhaps despise them? Was she growing or had she grown smug? She wriggled uncomfortably in the chair. The way he had spoken to her was like a benevolent but exasperated father.

Catching her breath, she examined the thoughts that flooded her mind. Was that why he had spoken like that? Did he see himself as her father?

After all, he had gone out of his way to be nice to them, particularly to her mother, Jon thought as she sat alone. Could he be planning to marry her? She had already wondered, and now the way he had spoken to her . . .

Suppose one day Alex was her stepfather? she asked herself. Would she mind?

It was a strange question to answer. Did she like him? Sometimes she did. At others she hated him. Maybe it wouldn't be so bad if he stopped calling her little Jon, but that was obviously how he saw her: as Uncle Ned's 'little Jon'. Perhaps she was being oversensitive about it? Maybe she should try to see him differently, ignore his teasing and be more friendly. After all, if he was going to marry her mother . . .'

When he returned, she smiled at him. 'Alex, why do people keep asking me if I'm going to sell the farm? That's another thing. What is the name of the farm? Mr Williams did tell me, but I've forgotten.'

He sat down, stretching out his long legs as he handed her the ice cream. 'The name is Jabula. It means happy.'

'Jabula. Jabula,' Jon repeated. 'It's rather nice. Was Uncle Ned so happy?'

'Yes, very happy, but only after he had battled with years of drought and hail and then people let him down, and then, quite suddenly, his luck changed and he managed to buy this farm on a mortgage, and he was so delighted with it that he called it Jabula.'

'And yours?'

'Mine was called Mukwene. That means a big mountain. Now it's known as the Wild Life Sanctuary.' He smiled. 'Are you interested in titles? Madeleine's father's farm is named Pumula. That means peace, but anything farther removed from a peaceful atmosphere would be hard to find!'

'Why?'

He shook his head. 'You'll be invited there to dinner and can see what I mean. Incidentally, our dorp is called Somahaha. That causes some laughter.'

'Somahaha? Why?'

He smiled. 'So-ma-ha-ha,' he said slowly.

She laughed. Some of the tension she had felt before was leaving her.

'Our nearest town, which isn't very large, is called Qwaleni. Odd names to you, I suppose, but . . .' He paused and gave her a wry smile. 'Dare I say you'll get used to it, or shall I have my head bitten off for saying those words?'

'I'm sorry,' she said, embarrassed, 'I didn't mean to. I'm a bit edgy.' She leaned forward, suddenly able to confide in him. 'You see, I have so much to learn and sometimes I wonder if I ever will live up to Uncle Ned's trust in me. He must have believed I could run the farm or else he would have sold it and left me the money.'

'Smoke?' Alex asked, and added, 'No, of course you don't. Know something, Jon? Your uncle was a crafty old devil. When he made a plan and set his heart on it, he had an amazing knack of getting what he wanted done and in his own way. He obviously wanted you to have the chance to be completely independent and to learn to stand on your own feet. So he left you the farm.'

'He didn't want to sell it?'

'No.' Alex hesitated and Jon had the feeling

that he was not sure whether to tell her more. However, he seemed to have made up his mind, for he leaned forward. 'When I needed more land for my Sanctuary I offered to buy this farm. He refused to sell it. I happen to know that a number of others wanted to buy the farm, too, but he always said No.'

'Why?'

'Because he wanted to give it to you.' He looked round and Jon saw that the cricketers were slowly walking out to the pitch; the children, shouting and laughing, were making for the pool, followed by their mothers.

Alex stood up. Jon looked up at him. What should she do when he left her? Pretend to watch cricket? It had always bored her unless she knew the players personally, and then everything was different.

But Alex spoke to her. 'I want to talk to you alone, Jon, so let's go to the car where we can't be disturbed.'

'But . . .' Jon hesitated, 'I can't just leave Mum.'

He smiled. 'She's in good hands and we won't be long. Come.' He caught hold of her hand and pulled her to her feet, still holding her hand tightly as he led the way to the parked cars. She went with him, for everyone would have seen had she struggled to free herself. But she felt worried, for what could he have to say to her that was so private?

He drove back to the main road and then

fast along the empty roads, finally making his way through an avenue of trees that looked so beautiful, the sun shimmering through the green leaves and throwing shadows on the red earth road.

Alex stopped by the side of a narrow stream that was tumbling down over some rocks.

'This is the Hluti river. I'm lucky, because it runs through my land,' he said as he opened the car door for Jon.

They sat on the rocks, a little above the river. He took an envelope out of his pocket and handed it to her.

'Your uncle gave me this some months before his illness got so much worse. He made me promise to give it to you *alone*.' He paused, looking at her gravely. 'On no account, he said, must your mother see it.'

Jon looked worried. 'But that isn't very nice.'

'She wasn't very nice to him.'

Staring at the man by her side, Jon was furious. How dared he speak like that about her mother? And yet he was right. That was the worst part of it.

'Open it.'

Her hands were shaking as she obeyed. Then, before she took out the letter, she stood up and moved away.

Alex laughed, 'I wasn't going to look over your shoulder.'

'Uncle Ned wanted this to be a secret.'

Shaking his head, Alex smiled. 'You're wrong, as usual, little Jon. He said nothing about me. Only that your mother must not see it.'

'All the same . . .' she said, hating him, for it was true. As usual he was right.

'All right.' He laughed and swung round so that his back was turned to her.

She opened the letter and read it slowly. Then she read it again. And again.

'My dear little Jon, I hope you will be as happy at Jabula as I have been. I know that your dream was to have mountains and water near you. This is the perfect life. Alex will help you run the farm if you find it too difficult at first. He is a good man, little Jon, and my best friend. You can trust him. Only one thing, please. Alex wants to buy the farm, but don't ever *sell* it to him.'

The word *sell* was heavily underlined. What did he mean? That she could sell the farm to anyone but Alex? It didn't make sense, for Uncle Ned also said Alex was to be trusted.

She tore the letter up into tiny pieces and threw them in the water, watching them float away. And why mustn't her mother see the letter?

'Well?' said Alex, sounding amused as he saw the paper drifting away. 'Was it so important?'

Jon looked at him thoughtfully. There must be a reason, though she could not see it. 'Yes,' she said quietly. 'Very important indeed.'

CHAPTER FOUR

As the days passed, Jon realized one thing—one simple but disagreeable fact that had to be accepted: that she could not manage the farm alone!

What upset her most was the thought that she was letting down her Uncle Ned. He had given her the farm, trusting her, believing in her, and although she was doing her best, she knew she could not cope alone. She was forever asking questions of the farmers she knew, borrowing books from Alex, disciplining herself to ignore his amused looks, so she had tried very hard, she tried to comfort herself one beautiful early morning as she took her daily walk with the dogs, amused by their excited leaps and explorations of the rows and rows of pineapple plants.

It was very hot even at this early hour and as she walked along the red earth, deeply indented by the wheel marks of the heavy tractors, she wished there had been trees planted occasionally to give some shade, but even so, she was so lost in admiration of the mountains that small irritations like the fruit flies, and the zooming whirl of mosquitoes who always sounded so triumphant, for she was constantly bitten, could not spoil her happiness. It was so wonderfully quiet that a serenity seemed to fill her. It was so quiet, she thought again, and suddenly the impatient chugging of a tractor destroyed the stillness and her happiness seemed to go.

Her dreaminess vanished and she became practical, looking back down the days that had become weeks, and none of them had been easy. On some of the days her mother was full of woe; complaining of the mosquitoes, the noisy chatter of the servants, the television she missed, the fact that she had nothing to do.

Jon had tried to tease her out of her despondency.

'You always wanted to be a lady of leisure, Mum. Now you are one. You remember how you hated working at that hotel?'

But her mother didn't laugh. 'At least there I met people.'

'But you are here. You're learning to play bowls and bridge,' Jon would say.

And her mother would look at her. 'It's not the same.' And Jon would go off for a walk with the dogs despite the heat as she tried not to be depressed. She loved Jabula so much. This was her home, but if her mother . . . ?

Then the next day everything would change. The phone would ring and her mother would answer and turn away, her face bright and eager. 'Jon darling, Mrs Hamilton is fetching me after lunch to go to the W.I.'

'I could have driven you there,' Jon would say, and her mother would smile: 'I prefer to go with someone, darling. You know how I hate walking in alone.'

Now, remembering all this as she walked through the pineapple lands, Jon sighed, picking up a piece of wood and flinging it ahead for the dogs to race after. In many ways, her mother was still her biggest problem, but so was Alex too.

Make no mistake, Jon told herself sternly, you have no right whatsoever to resent Alex, because you owe him so much.

And that, she knew very well, was the trouble. If only . . .

She turned suddenly, giving the distant hazy blue mountains a last loving look, and slowly retraced her steps, as it must be nearly breakfast time. Her thoughts were still in the past as she remembered the first Monday morning they had been there. After a long day at the club, she had slept heavily. Alex's voice had awakened her. Drowsily she had glanced at her small alarm clock. It was only half past four! What on earth was he doing here at that time? she had wondered as she tumbled out of bed, pulled on her thin green dressing-gown and gone to the window, pulling back the curtain so that she could see. It was light, the sky a strange mixture of colours, and Alex was there, on a black horse, as he talked to her *induna*, obviously giving him his orders for the day. And then Alex had turned and ridden away and she had gone back to bed, not to sleep but lie awake thinking of him and how sarcastic he could be, and yet at other times so sympathetic. Did every farmer's day start at four-thirty? she wondered. Would she have to learn to get up at that hour? What sort of orders would she give? Could she ever learn the local language?

That first Monday was one she would never forget, for later that morning she had gone outside with the dogs and found Leonard cleaning a car.

She stared at it and then felt annoyed with herself. She should have known that Uncle Ned had got a car. After all, you could not live here without one, as well as the two trucks and various tractors and other vehicles. Alex had waved a hand vaguely at where they were parked under a tin roof.

The car was dark grey and had long graceful lines. She walked round it, running her hand over the polished surface almost tenderly, for it was Uncle Ned's. She would take good care of it, she promised silently.

Then Alex's voice had come. 'Never seen a car before?'

Startled, she swung round, almost falling over, having to grab at the car to save herself. How had Alex got there? She had heard no car, no horse, not even his footsteps. How long had he been watching her? she wondered.

'I had my own car in England,' she said stiffly.

'You did?' His amused, almost sceptical voice reminded her of Madeleine's reaction at that first dinner party. Why must they both always treat her as a child? Jon had thought angrily.

'Drive me round for a while,' Alex said that first Monday morning, opening the car door, telling Leonard to finish cleaning the car later. 'Driving out here is different from driving in England.'

'I'm sure it's quite unnecessary to give you a demonstration,' Jon had begun stiffly, but of course, and as usual, Alex won and she had driven him.

Walking towards the house as she remembered that morning, she smiled ruefully remembering the miserable hour she had spent driving Alex. A strange car, different gears, a more powerful car than she had been used to, learning to drive over the corrugations in the roads, crawling carefully to start with because she was concerned about the car, and then scolded by Alex and told the only way was to drive over the corrugations fast! She could do nothing right, of course. He had asked her about the road signs; many of them were different from those at home. He lectured her on driving on muddy roads, explaining about skids, warning her that, in no circumstances, must she give anyone she didn't know a lift.

Then, when they returned, he had smiled at her.

'Not bad at all,' he had said in that hateful patronizing voice. 'Why were you scared stiff? Am I such an ogre?'

She had managed to laugh but avoided looking at him in case he had recognized the truth, for in a sense, he was an ogre! He gave her an inferiority complex one moment, the next he infuriated her. It had been an ordeal, for driving a car with a critic by your side is rather like typing with someone watching you. No matter how good you are, then you're bound to make stupid mistakes.

But that morning before she had had time to answer him, Madeleine had come round the corner.

'I wondered where you were, Alex,' she had greeted him, totally ignoring Jon. Madeleine was wearing cream shorts and thin blue blouse, her hair hanging down her back. 'I thought I could help Jon as regards shopping and coping with the staff as she isn't used to servants.'

Alex had given her a strange smile, Jon remembered, and she still could not understand it. 'How very thoughtful of you. Goodbye, Jon,' was all he said and then he had left them.

That had been the first of Madeleine's daily visits. Walking along the red earth track, the dogs racing eagerly ahead, Jon looked back on those visits. Maybe Madeleine had meant it

70

kindly and, to be honest, she had been a great help, driving Jon to the local dorp, introducing her to the young couple who ran the store so efficiently, introducing Jon to local people so that Jon's daily visit to the store was something her mother, who always went with her, looked forward to. This was something her mother needed, Jon realized, she needed people to talk to! Jon didn't.

She was near the house when she heard her mother's voice and then Alex's. Half hidden by a huge Pride of India bush, Jon paused, aware that she must look hot and sticky, and not feeling inclined to see Alex.

Her mother's voice came, clear and musical.

'Please be patient, Alex. It may take time, but she'll change her mind. I know Jon so well.'

Jon caught her breath. She despised people who eavesdropped, but she had done it unintentionally. If she walked round the bush, they would see her and know she had heard! Alex might even accuse her of snooping! Her mother would be horribly embarrassed. There was only one solution, so Jon turned quickly, walking towards the back door and going into the house through the kitchen, then quietly into the bathroom for a shower. Perhaps when she came out, Alex would have gone.

In any case, why had he come? And what had her mother meant? Jon asked herself as the tepid water bounced off her hot sticky skin.

'Please be patient, Alex. It may take time, but she'll change her mind. I know Jon so well.'

They could only have been discussing her, Jon decided. And why had her mother said 'she'll change her mind'?

A sickening fear seized Jon. It could only mean one thing: that Alex and her mother wanted the farm sold—and that her mother was on Alex's side. Tears were very near as she went over the words again and again. How could her mother do this when she knew how much Jabula meant to her daughter.

Turning on the cold tap, Jon shivered as the cold water hit her skin, but she let it pour over her body, trying to fight her dismay, gradually persuading herself that she was quite wrong and that her mother only wanted to help her. Maybe her mother realized—as Jon now had—that she could not cope with the farm herself. Maybe it was Alex who had persuaded her mother that this would be for Jon's good?

Jon turned off the water and rubbed herself dry. As she dressed quickly, she felt a new strength filling her. She must find a way to prove that she *could* run the farm without Alex's aid.

Suddenly she knew the answer. Why hadn't she realized it before? It was a simple but perfect answer to her problem.

Many of the farms around them had similar problems. Owners who lived far away and could not be on the spot to cope—they found a solution. The solution she could have.

Jon knew what she would do. That morning when she took her mother in to Qwaleni to buy some thinner dresses, she would slip away and put an advertisement in the local newspaper.

The answer to her problems? A good manager.

That was all she needed, and he would free her from this awful dependence on Alex!

*　　　*　　　*

When Jon joined her mother on the stoep, she saw with relief that Alex had gone. Her mother looked up from the magazine she was reading.

'You're late. I'm longing for my breakfast.'

Jon sat down. 'Sorry. I must have walked farther than I meant to and I was so hot I had to shower. You shouldn't have waited for me.'

'Of course I had to. You know how I hate eating alone.'

There was an awkward silence. Jon wondered why her mother had not mentioned Alex's visit. Then the little bell from the dining room tinkled and they went in to eat. But there were moments of awkward silence during the meal and Jon hated it, for she loathed this sort of secrecy.

'By the way, Jon,' her mother said after one long silence, 'I'll be out all day. Mrs Swayne is

73

coming to fetch me this morning and I'm having lunch with her and then playing bowls. This evening she's taking me to dinner with the Cartwrights and we're going to play bridge.'

Jon tried to hide her dismay. 'I thought you wanted me to take you to Qwaleni?'

'We can go another day. There's no hurry to get those dresses. I thought you'd be glad, because I know how you hate that drive.'

That was true, she did, Jon thought as she took a second piece of toast, but at the same time, now that she had decided to advertise for a farm manager, she didn't want to waste any time. That day would be the last for getting the advertisement into this week's paper.

'All the same, I think I'll go in,' she said casually.

'But why, Jon? You can go in with me another day. Or have you a specific reason for going in?' There was a new, almost accusing note in her mother's voice.

'No. I just feel like going in today,' Jon said, hoping her mother wouldn't notice her tell-tale blush.

Her mother shrugged. 'You are a funny girl, Jon. Sometimes I just can't understand you.'

Jon felt tempted to say 'But you just told Alex you knew me so well!' but how could she mention Alex's visit unless her mother did, and if the whole thing came out into the open, there might be one of those emotional scenes

74

with her mother that she dreaded and that left Ursula exhausted for days.

Mrs Swayne arrived in her black car and Jon waved them goodbye, then wandered round the house. She could hear the chugging of the tractors, the sudden crow of a cock, the chatter of Violet and Dorcas in the kitchen, and she thought how much she loved the sounds. This was her home. Her beloved home.

Jon felt restless, wishing there was someone with whom she could discuss the situation. Part of her was eager to rush in to Qwaleni and put the advertisement in the newspaper—another part of her hesitated. Was she doing the right thing? Should she consult Alex?

She went out on the stoep, the dogs leaping up excitedly as they thought that meant a walk, then as she sank into a chair, they sat down close by, looking at her with reproachful eyes.

But Jon hardly noticed them for once. She was thinking of Alex. If she told him she wanted to get a farm manager, she could imagine the light of triumph in his eyes. Even if he didn't say: 'I told you so', he would make it obvious that it was what he thought!

Then she felt ashamed. Was she unjust? Uncle Ned had said she was to trust Alex.

Yet she must not sell the farm to him. It didn't make sense. What should she do?

The sound of a car brought her to her feet. Was it Alex? she wondered. No, it was Madeleine! Getting out of her car with her usual gracefulness, hurrying across the sunlit lawn in a brief white frock, looking as beautiful as usual. But she happened to be the very last person Jon wanted to see at that moment!

'Is Alex here?' Madeleine asked curtly without any greeting.

'As far as I know he isn't unless he's out on the lands, but then he usually lets us know.'

'Where's your mother?'

'Gone out with Mrs Swayne.'

Madeleine frowned. 'Alex hasn't been here at all?'

Jon hesitated. 'I took the dogs for a walk before breakfast and he wasn't here when I got back.'

'Your mother said nothing?'

'No, she didn't,' Jon snapped, suddenly annoyed. What right had Madeleine to come and question her like this?

Madeleine looked startled. 'I'm sorry if this seems a cross-examination, Jon, I didn't mean it that way.' Her voice became almost placating. 'Only I've been trying to get Alex on the phone since it came on and no one seems to know where he is.' She smiled sweetly, but somehow Jon distrusted the smile. A sudden idea came to her. Was Madeleine jealous? Had she, too, perhaps thought that Jon's mother and Alex . . .? After all, they were only a few years apart in age, and nowadays, few people worried about that! Poor Madeleine, so beautiful, so possessive and so sure of herself.

76

Would this explain her sudden appearance and abrupt and even rude manner?

'Would you like a cup of coffee?' Jon asked politely, hoping Madeleine would refuse. But she didn't.

'Lovely idea.' Madeleine sat down in one of the cane chairs. 'By the way, Jon, Mother asked me to ask you if your ma and you would come to dinner tomorrow night?'

Jon, pausing on her way to the kitchen to tell Violet to make two cups of coffee, hesitated. She had no desire to go to Madeleine's home, the one Alex had joked about, saying it was called Pumula, which meant peace, and that peace was the last thing you got in the Cox home.

'I'll have to ask Mum, Madeleine. She's getting such a busy social life these days.'

They both laughed. 'She likes it, Jon?'

Jon nodded. 'Very much. She's dining out tonight and . . .'

A cloud seemed to descend over Madeleine's face. 'Tonight? Oh, is she?' Madeleine paused and Jon seized the chance to escape to the kitchen, knowing that Madeleine had wanted to ask with whom her mother was dining! Not that she would tell her. Certainly not; it was none of Madeleine's business.

Over coffee, they talked of various things such as the heat and the urgent need for rain. Also, of course, they talked of Alex. Of course,

Jon thought bitterly, all conversations inevitably ended up with Alex!

'I can't understand him,' Madeleine was saying, 'wasting his money on his wild life sanctuary. He's absolutely obsessed about it. He wants to make it bigger, you know.'

'Yes, I do know,' Jon said quietly. She waited for Madeleine to say something about selling Jabula—but she didn't!

'He works far too hard, of course. He never has a spare moment.' She looked at Jon and smiled. 'You're a nuisance, too, but I expect he's told you so.'

Jon's face burned. 'A nuisance?'

Madeleine laughed. 'Of course you are. Alex is worried stiff about you and your mother being here on your own. Do you know that this house is the one that has been burgled more often than any other in the valley?'

Jon caught her breath. How thankful she was that her mother wasn't with them! 'He didn't tell me.'

'Of course he didn't, or you'd be scared stiff, but every night he sends a boy down to see that all is well here, and every morning, as you know, he's here at dawn, giving your staff their jobs. It's like running a farm for no pay at all. That's typical of Alex. He's soft-hearted. The fuss he made of your uncle when he was ill! Anyone would have thought the man was a relation.'

'They were good friends.'

'Maybe, but there's a limit to the demands of friendship. I mean, let's face it, Jon, you haven't a hope of running this farm alone and you know it. You're just wasting Alex's time by your stubbornness.'

'Stubbornness?'

Madeleine nodded, her fair hair swinging forward.

'That's all it is. You're the laughing-stock of the neighbourhood. We all know you can't manage alone. A farm like this needs a man. Besides, you've no experience, no training—not a clue. I suppose your idea is to raise the price? Bleed poor generous Alex to death.'

Jon's temper was barely under control. 'I shall never—ever—sell Jabula to Alex, and that's for sure!'

Madeleine looked amused. 'If Alex stopped helping you—and I can assure you that he's fed to the teeth with doing so—you'd have no option. Alex will give you a better price than any other man. You'd be a fool to turn down his offer.'

Jon stood up. 'Fool or not, I mean what I said. I shall never—but never—sell the farm to Alex. I've told him so.'

'Why not?'

'Because . . .' Jon drew a deep breath, trying to control her anger. 'Because I love it here. Uncle Ned left it to me.'

'And you'll let it go smash? All his work

wasted? It will become a ruin. One day . . .' she laughed, 'one day it might be known as Uncle Ned's Ruin!'

'I shall never let it go smash,' Jon's voice was unsteady. 'Now, I don't want to be unsociable, Madeleine, but I've got to go in to Qwaleni this morning and . . .'

'I'm in the way?' Madeleine laughed. 'All right, but give me a ring about dinner tomorrow night. The parents want to meet you.'

I'm sure they do, Jon thought bitterly. She was the laughing-stock of the neighbourhood. They were all watching her, waiting for her to collapse and meekly sell the farm to Alex. Well, they could wait for ever—it was the very last thing she would do!

When Madeleine had gone, Jon hastily changed into a clean green frock. Her mind was no longer at doubt. She was doing the right thing—indeed, the only thing. No longer need poor Alex slave to help her—and then tell her neighbours how fed-up he was with helping her! Nor need he worry about them at night—*if* Madeleine's story of the burglars was true—for there would be a man about the house.

Qwaleni was thirty-five miles away and not a bad road, though only some of it was tarmac. She didn't enjoy the drive very much, but her urgent need to get to the local newspaper urged her on. She looked at everything she passed, thinking how the tribal clothing worn by many of the Africans had a dignity of its own. She liked the brightly coloured squares of cotton they wore. The men wore a square knotted on one shoulder while another piece of material hung like a kilt round his waist, the tail of an animal hanging down his back. His hair swept back, often whitened and with a feather. But most of the Africans wore trousers and shirts; working on the lands they wore their oldest clothes, of course, often torn and ragged.

Driving by the large market where the African women squatted or sat behind the stalls, she wondered how the babies, tied to their mothers' backs with blankets, could survive the heat of the sun on their faces. The babies' legs were stretched far apart, their little heads nodding as they slept peacefully. Sometimes a mother would walk along, holding a bright yellow or red sunshade over her head to shelter the baby. The women had such strength that often Jon would stare, wondering how they walked so upright with enormous cases balanced on their head, also carrying bundles and perhaps with a small child hanging on to his mother's skirt.

As Jon drove up the winding curved mountain road, she saw that huge white clouds were moving slowly, almost ruthlessly across the pale blue sky. They seemed to be threatening the beauty of everything for the great dark shadows, reflections of the clouds, were hiding the mountains' real colour and making them look almost dark purple. She hoped there wouldn't be a storm, but at least she had only one thing to do in Qwaleni—go to the local newspaper office. She sighed. Perhaps she had better do some shopping in case her mother asked questions. How she hated this deceitfulness! Once you got involved . . .

At least, she thought, as she gazed from the mountain top down on to the sprawling town below, she was doing something to solve the problem, something constructive! The problem? She laughed ruefully. What else but Alex?

The town was more crowded than she had expected and she had difficulty in parking the car. Then she walked down the main road, glancing at the shops, looking for the newspaper office. She could not find it, and after walking up and down the short high street twice, she went into a shop and bought some apples and tomatoes, then asked the Portuguese man the way to the newspaper office.

He told her. Finally it turned out to be just out of town and quite a walk. She had not realized how far it would be and wished she had taken the car as she walked along the red sandy road with few trees and in the scorching sunshine. However, at last she found the building, but then, as she went in, realized with dismay that she had not worked out the advertisement and hadn't a clue as to what to say.

Fortunately she was served by a friendly woman who was also new to the neighbourhood, to Jon's relief, for Madeleine's words that she was the 'laughing-stock of the neighbourhood' still hurt.

'You want a farm manager?' the assistant said. 'Then have a box number, otherwise you'll have them walking in on you. It's easier to sort out the no-goods by letter.'

'You think I'll have no difficulty in . . .'

'Getting one? Certainly not,' the red-headed woman laughed, 'so long as you pay a good salary. Do you want a married man or single?'

Jon looked startled. 'Does it make any difference?'

'It does when it comes to accommodation. A married man with a family would need a house.'

Thinking fast, Jon remembered something. 'There is a guest cottage, but it needs repainting and . . . well, actually I thought the farm manager could live with my mother and me and . . .'

'It might work and it might not. Only time will tell. So we'll say preferably a single man. We won't say where the farm is. That you can tell them when they write to you.'

Half an hour later, Jon went out into the hot

sunshine. She felt much happier. She had taken her first constructive step. By the time she reached the shops and her parked car, the perspiration was running down her face, her clothes sticking to her wet body, her feet sore, her head aching. She longed for a cool shower as she unlocked the car door and was about to slide in when a voice stopped her.

'What on earth are you doing here, little Jon?'

She swung round, startled. 'Sh—shopping, Alex.'

His eyes narrowed. 'You've been a long time. I've been waiting here for you.' He glanced up at the clouds, now blacker than before and seeming much lower. 'Have you got much else to do, as we ought to get going. There's going to be a big storm.'

'I'll be all right. You don't have to worry . . .'

'That's what you think,' Alex said coldly. 'I know better. I'll follow you home.'

She stared at him, so angry she could not speak. Then she remembered that it wouldn't be long before she would be freed from his constant interference, and inside her, she felt triumphant.

'All right,' she said, her voice meek. 'I'm going now.'

How she hated that drive home! She was so painfully conscious of his much more powerful car behind her. She made so many stupid mistakes; ones she always blamed others for if they did them, but today she was making them herself—overtaking when she should have been more cautious, forgetting to signal a turn. If only his car would break down or she could surge ahead and be out of his sight! Why must she always go to pieces when he was around?

She knew one truth—that she wanted him to praise her, that she wanted to be a woman and not a little Jon! Why, she asked herself wearily, why did it matter so much to her what Alex thought?

They were on top of the last mountain when the storm broke. The rain was like a grey sheet, cutting out the view, making the windscreen wipers seem useless. It was hard to see ahead, even though the cars had their lights on. The sky was rent by zig-zag jagged flashes of lightning, showing brightly in the dark clouds. Terrific cracks of thunder shattered the air as Jon clung to the steering wheel, peering ahead as the car skidded in the mud, and she wished it was a tarmac road. It didn't help to know that on one side of the mountain there was a sheer drop of thousands of feet. Everything was grey and strangely cold.

She tried to remember all that Alex had told her about driving in bad weather and as the nightmare of the drive grew worse and mist enveloped them so she had to crawl along, looking anxiously for the glow of lights from approaching cars, she really wondered if she should sell the farm. Was this the sort of life she could cope with? These terrifying storms, the terrible roads . . .

But there again, that unanswerable question came up: Why had Uncle Ned said the farm must never be sold to Alex Roe?

'Why?' she asked herself. If only she knew!

As she drove down towards the valley, the rain ceased and the clouds moved away, and by the time she reached the valley the roads were dry, the sun shining. All the same, she was glad to see Jabula and even more glad as she drove into the open garage and switched off the engine.

She sat still for a moment. What a nightmare it had been! Now, as she got out of the car and the two dogs came bounding to meet her, she saw Alex drive in. She was surprised, for she had thought he would drive on past to his own home. Perhaps she should thank him for his consideration, for maybe it had even upset his plans.

'Alex . . .' she began as he strode towards her, but he spoke at the same time.

'Congratulations,' he smiled. 'You did darned well.'

She could not believe it! Alex praising her! Then he added: 'Considering it was your first storm.'

Some of the pleasure caused by his words vanished. Why must he spoil everything?

'I was terrified,' she confessed.

He smiled again. 'Aren't we all, especially

the first time. It's not a pleasant experience, Jon, but in time one learns how to cope. Next time you won't find it so hard.'

She ran her hand through her hair. 'I hope not. I'm exhausted.'

'What you need is a cold drink and something to eat. So do I.' He glanced at his watch and whistled softly. 'Any idea of the time?'

'None.' Jon looked at hers and gasped. 'Why, it's nearly three! You'll have missed your lunch.'

'And you yours. Can't I share it? What are you having?'

'Just cold meat and salad.' Jon hesitated. 'Mum is out,' she added, thinking that he might have suggested staying to lunch in order to see her mother.

He grinned at that. 'So what? Afraid there'll be a local scandal because we lunch alone?'

She went red. 'Of course not. I just thought . . .'

'Well, I'm hungry, so why are we wasting time?' He took her arm and led the way up the steps to the stoep. 'Go and shout for Violet and I'll get the cold drinks.'

She obeyed, stopping briefly in the bathroom and surveying her flushed face with a frown for her hair was rumpled and her nose shiny.

'Jon!' Alex called.

'Coming!' Jon shouted back, giving a little

shrug. It would be a waste of time trying to make herself look attractive with two people as lovely as her mother and Madeleine around. In any case, Alex never even 'saw' her; she was merely 'little Jon', the niece of his best friend.

As they ate lunch, Alex asked abruptly: 'Is your mother feeling happier here?'

Suddenly wary, Jon looked up. 'Definitely,' she said and hoped he had not heard the note of defiance in her voice.

'I thought so this morning,' Alex went on, his tone casual. 'I'm glad she's making so many friends, because she needs friends, you know, Jon. She's not a loner like you.'

Jon's mouth was dry. 'You . . . you were here this morning?'

'Yes, you were out with the dogs. I just looked in.' He stared at her for what seemed an endless moment. 'Didn't your mother tell you I looked in?'

Jon shook her head silently. Had he seen her walking towards the house? Had he seen her hesitate and turn hurriedly away? Would he make her lie and then tell her that he knew that she'd heard what her mother had said.

'She didn't tell me.' At least, Jon thought, she could say that truthfully.

'It wasn't about anything important. This is good meat, Jon. Which butcher did you go to?' he asked, and the conversation changed as they discussed the difficulties of shopping, the necessity of having a deep-freeze, and it wasn't until they were on the stoep, drinking coffee, that Jon became wary again, for Alex said casually: 'I was surprised to see your car in Qwaleni this morning. You see, I'd told your mother I was going in and she said you had been taking her in but her plans had changed. She was so sure you wouldn't go in alone, as you hate the drive. What made you change your mind?'

Jon tried to think quickly. Alex mustn't find out about the advertisement for the farm manager until it had all been settled.

'I felt restless. I hadn't anything much to do.'

He looked amused. 'Don't tell me you're getting bored? I thought you loved the quiet simplicity of your new life.'

'Of course I do, but . . .' Jon stopped herself in time, for it would be a mistake to let him make her lose her temper.

Alex stood up. 'I must go. I've wasted enough time already today. What you need is a husband and six children little Jon, then you wouldn't have time to feel restless.' He smiled down at her. 'Seen Madeleine?'

'Yes. She came here this morning, looking for you.'

'I told her yesterday that I was going to Qwaleni today. She never remembers anything. Did she remember to invite you both to dinner tomorrow?'

'Yes.'

'You're going, of course.'

'Well, I don't know about Mum . . .'

'She wants to go. I asked her this morning. She hasn't a very high opinion of Madeleine, has she? How do you get on with her?'

'With Madeleine? All right, but . . .'

'But . . .?' There was a strange note in Alex's voice. Was it anger, exasperation, or irritation? Jon wondered. She stood up. She hated it when he towered above her and it made it a million times worse when she was sitting down.

'We get on all right, but we're not close friends, Alex. You know that very well.'

'She wants to be friends. She needs one badly.'

'Does she? That isn't the impression I get, Alex.' He looked surprised. 'I don't understand.'

Jon moved impatiently. 'Of course you do. Madeleine is the most beautiful girl I've ever seen, but she never lets me forget it. And it's I . . . I . . . I . . . all the time. She's been most helpful, but I'm sure it was only because you told her to be.'

'You think she'd obey me? Just like that?' Alex was smiling, openly amused by Jon's outburst.

'You know very well she'd do anything you told her to.'

He laughed. 'I'm flattered. I don't think you know Madeleine very well. She suffers from an outsize inferiority complex.'

'Madeleine?' Jon stared at him. 'That I can't believe.'

He shrugged. 'Well, she does.'

'But . . .'

'You'll understand better after you've been to her home. I'm sorry for the girl.'

'Sorry—for Madeleine? You're teasing me,' Jon said.

'Why should I waste my valuable time teasing you?' Alex asked with a smile, lifted his hand and said goodbye. 'See you tomorrow, then,' he said casually, and walked off to his car.

Jon waited until the car was out of sight and then she sat down, ignoring for once the loving tongues of the two dogs as they moved round her, trying to persuade her to take them for a walk.

'Wasting his valuable time,' Alex had said. Wasn't that just what Madeleine had said, too? So he must have said those very words to her and she merely repeated them. Had he, perhaps, told Madeleine to tell Jon? Well, she thought angrily, soon he wouldn't have to waste his valuable time. Soon she would have her own farm manager and be quite independent. Perhaps then people would stop laughing at her and waiting for her to give in and admit failure. Perhaps the laughter and watching was due to Alex's . . .? Well, they were all due for a big surprise. Nothing—but nothing was going to make her give up the farm. Nothing whatsoever.

Rex began to whine, rolling over on his back and waving his legs, then leaping to his feet, barking excitedly.

Jon laughed. 'All right, all right!' she told the dogs. 'Let me just change my shoes and we'll go for a walk.'

The well-known beloved word brought them both to life as they raced up and down the stoep, barking impatiently until Jon was ready.

She walked slowly down the track, a light hat on her head. She had so much to think about. The two dogs leapt about and raced far ahead, occasionally looking to make sure she was following them and then rushing off again. The spaniel, Jock, walked behind her, still ignoring her but no longer avoiding her, even wagging his tail when she stroked him. Maybe he was accepting her in a minor way, but she still was not his beloved Uncle Ned.

Jon thought of her uncle, wishing she had known him better, wishing for the thousandth time at least that her mother would stop blaming him for something he was not guilty of doing. She also wished she could tell her mother that it had been Uncle Ned financing them for those nine years, without any expectation of gratitude or friendliness from them.

She also wished she could understand her

uncle's letter. Why couldn't her mother read it? And why could the farm be sold, but not to Alex?

If only she could understand the real Alex! Sometimes she would think him sympathetic, even kind, and then instantly he would change, openly laughing at her.

And how odd that he should say Madeleine suffered from an inferiority complex? How could she, when she looked so lovely?

And why—another question came into Jon's mind—why had her mother been so silent at breakfast? Why not have said Alex had looked in and that they'd been invited to dinner at Pumula? Surely she couldn't have forgotten it in that short time? Then her mother had also known Alex was going into Qwaleni? Why hadn't she said so? For that matter so had Madeleine known and she had said nothing

Jon rubbed her face wearily and yawned, for it was too hot to walk far. She saw the mountains ahead and the clouds were coming in fast and low, hiding the green pastures and grey-blue rocks. She called the dogs, turned and walked back to the empty house. She could hear music from the radio in the girls' rooms and their laughter, but as she went from room to room of the house before having her shower, she tried to think of her uncle living here alone, always alone.

Showering, she wondered what Alex had meant when he called her a 'loner'. Hadn't he once before said the same about Uncle Ned? What exactly was a loner?

As she rubbed herself dry, she decided that maybe he meant that she and Uncle Ned were rarely lonely and preferred not to be one of a crowd. In England she had had her friends, but she didn't *need* them.

Putting on a clean frock, she thought of Madeleine. How could she need a friend? In any case, after the way she had spoken that morning, it was obvious that Madeleine had no friendly feelings for the rooinek—the 'laughing-stock' of the neighbourhood!

Dressed, Jon went into the guest room of the house. Would it be suitable for the farm manager? she wondered. She could get him a table or desk to go under the window. She could move in an armchair from the lounge. There was a bedside lamp. The colour scheme was leaf-green, quite attractive. Would he consider it big enough? He need only have his meals with them, of course. It seemed an excellent plan, for her mother would be much happier, knowing a man was sleeping in the house to protect them.

She went back to the stoep, wondering what sort of applications for the job she would get. She must choose wisely or else Alex would have another opportunity to make fun of her.

How quiet it was! For once there were no noisy tractors, but the clouds were getting lower and coming closer. Now there was only a small part of the sky that was still blue, touched with a faint tinge of pink, reminding her that it was later than she had realized and that soon the sun would go down.

She went out to the kitchen and told Violet there would only be one person for dinner. Not feeling hungry, she changed her mind, telling the girls they could go to their rooms and she would cook her own dinner. It would give her something to do, she teased herself as she got out her writing case. She'd scramble some eggs and add some tomatoes, since all she felt like was a light meal.

She was busy writing letters when suddenly a wind seemed to spring up from nowhere, making the curtains blow into the room and the doors and windows rattle. It was like a gale. Jon jumped up. The trees were being whipped savagely by the wind, bending almost to the ground. Even as she hurried round the house, closing the windows, shutting the doors, the electricity came on and she silently blessed Leonard for remembering to do it for the sun had gone down and everything was getting dark. At that moment the rain came.

Never had she seen such rain. It was even worse than it had been during the storm she met coming back from Qwaleni earlier that day. The hard rain beat into the ground so that it became mud almost instantly, making deep ruts through the garden. As Jon stood by the windows watching, she could see the havoc being played amongst the flowers as they were whipped out by the wind or beaten to the ground by the rain. A terrific clap of thunder filled the air and the room was bright with the flash of lightning. Jon moved rapidly away from the window and then felt ashamed of her fear. She hoped they were not having this bad storm where her mother was, for she, poor darling, was absolutely terrified.

So was she, Jon confessed, as the storm grew worse. Never had she seen such savagery as the sky was cut in half almost by the brilliant lightning while the thunder made a reverberating crash at the same instant. It was as if she was in the centre of it all, caged in, never to escape.

She swung round as the front door opened. The dogs heard nothing, all three of them had retired under the beds at the first noisy crash. She saw Alex, water dripping from him, his hair flattened, water running down his face as he took off his mackintosh.

'Okay?' he asked. 'I'll put this in the kitchen.'

When he came back she had not moved, then she swallowed and managed a smile. 'It was a bit frightening,' she confessed. 'I've never seen lightning like that before.'

'Shall we have a drink?' he asked, and went, without waiting for her reply, to Uncle Ned's circular bamboo 'bar'.

She sipped the drink he gave her and

though it burned her throat a little, it warmed her. She sat down and laughed uneasily.

'I know it's absurd, but I've . . . You know, Alex, I've never really minded a storm before.'

She had to shout, as the thunder was still crashing overhead and then rumbling away into the distance so that for a moment it seemed as if the storm was over, but suddenly another great crash overhead told them the storm was still with them.

Alex smiled, 'You'll get used to them.'

Jon found herself laughing. 'I wish I could be as optimistic as you. I just hate to think what poor Mum is going through. They terrify her even in England.'

'I expect they'll be too busy playing bridge to notice.' He glanced at his watch. 'Or else they'll be having dinner. You eaten yet?'

'No. I sent the girls off. I thought I'd scramble some eggs.'

Alex stood up. 'I'm starving. You've never tasted the famous Roe omelettes, so now's your chance. Just sit still, I know where everything is. Uncle Ned and I were great at cooking.' He chuckled. 'Just wait until you taste my omelettes! They're not easy to forget.'

How right he was, Jon thought, a half hour later when he brought in an enormous omelette with fried tomatoes. The storm seemed to be dying away, but the rain still beat wildly against the windows, streams of water running down the glass.

'Well,' Alex demanded, 'what's your verdict? Am I a good cook?'

Jon laughed, 'Absolutely perfect. After this, I'll never dare to cook anything for you!'

How strange he was, she thought. He did it all with such dignity. How she wished she had been there when he and Uncle Ned had played at being 'chef'.

The phone bell rang and Jon hesitated for a moment, but the storm seemed to have subsided. She answered and it was her mother.

'Jon darling, you are all right? I know how you hate thunderstorms.'

'Are *you* all right?' Jon asked, amused at the way her mother always implied that it was her daughter who was the scared one.

'I'm fine, darling, having a lovely time. I just rang to say I won't be home tonight.'

'What? I'm sorry, Mum, I didn't hear what you said.' But Jon had heard, every word.

'I said I can't get home tonight, darling. The river down here has flooded and the road's impassable. I hope to be up tomorrow. You'll be all right, of course. You've got the dogs.'

'Yes,' said Jon, her voice suddenly dull and lifeless, 'I've got the dogs.'

As she put down the receiver, there was another loud crash of thunder and the whole room was bright with lightning. Slowly she realized what it meant. That night she would be alone in the house that had been more often burgled than any in the valley! But she'd have the dogs. Of course. And she was a loner, as Alex had said. Besides it wasn't her mother's fault. Of course, Jon thought, she didn't mind. She'd be perfectly all right . . .

'Something wrong?' Alex's voice pierced her thoughts.

Jon's face felt stiff. 'No. Just that Mum can't get home tonight because the river's flooded.'

He stood up and collected the plates. 'I made some fruit salad. Okay?'

'It sounds wonderful,' she said dully.

Alone, she hugged herself, her arms round her body, as she had always done as a child when she was frightened. Don't be so silly, she told herself. After all, if her mother *was* there, what protection was she? Yet, of course, it was just knowing someone was there. But she would have the dogs . . .

Alex brought in the tray with the fruit salad. He sat down and they ate in silence, the thunder coming and going, almost rhythmically. Then he put down his plate and stretched out his legs, yawning.

'Well, it's been quite a day, so I suggest we make it an early night. I've got to be up soon after four tomorrow. I'm expecting the delivery of a young eagle.'

Jon nodded silently. She had hoped he wouldn't go just yet. Another mighty crash of thunder split the silence.

Jon stood up. 'It was very good of you to come, Alex. I'll get your mac.'

He smiled up at her. 'I'm not going, Jon. Do you think I'd leave you here on your own? This is your first bad storm.'

Her legs felt absurdly weak and she sat down. 'You're not . . . going?'

He smiled. 'Of course not. I've brought my toothbrush and razor.' He laughed. 'Don't look so shocked, little Jon. You ought to know you're safe with me. This is Africa, you know, and not a small market town. No one will know, and if they did, they'd think nothing of it.' He stood up, stretching his arms above his head and yawning. 'Mind if I have first bath? Put the sheets on the bed in the guest room. I can make the bed.' He came to stand by her, leaning down to tilt her head back with his hand. 'I'll be gone when you wake up in the morning, little Jon, but sleep well and don't be scared. The storm is all noise. We rarely get struck down here in the valley.'

He bent and kissed her, very gently. Then he was gone and she could hear the bath running and him whistling.

She sat very still for a moment, then stood up. Somehow she moved, forcing her limbs to obey, going to the linen cupboard, then taking the linen to the guest room, making up the bed, letting the dogs out for a last-minute run.

The rain was still teeming down, a curtain of grey water. She went to her bedroom, closed the door, and went to the mirror to gaze at herself.

Her eyes looked worriedly back at her.

'It can't be true,' she whispered. 'It just can't be true.'

But it was. She knew it was. Much later that night as she lay awake, no longer afraid of the thunder or of the bright white light that filled the room at intervals, no longer aware of anything except the truth.

The truth? That she was in love. In love with a man who saw her only as 'little Jon', the niece of his best friend.

In love with Alex.

CHAPTER FIVE

When Jon awoke, the sun was streaming into her room. She sat up quickly and Rex moved to her side to lick her hand.

'The wonderful thing about this country, Rex,' Jon said sleepily, 'is that even though it can rain like mad, you know the sun will shine.' She yawned happily, stretching her arms, and then, quite suddenly, she stiffened as she remembered!

Alex!

Her mouth was dry, her throat seemed to close so that, for a moment, she could hardly breathe.

Alex. He was here. He had been for the night and she had just discovered that she loved him, more than she had ever believed it possible to love. It couldn't be true! It mustn't. It only made everything even more complicated than before.

She slid out of bed, hurriedly pulling on jeans and a white shirt, then quietly opened her bedroom door. Now she must watch her every thought, be on guard against the chance of betraying her secret. Whatever happened, Alex must never know.

From her bedroom doorway, she could see the guest room. The door stood open. The bed was covered with the bedspread. The room looked as it always did, as if it had never been slept in. In the bathroom, she glanced into the linen basket. The sheets were there, and two pillow-slips, awaiting the wash-girl. Jon looked at her watch. It was barely six o'clock. Alex must have risen early and gone off so quietly that she didn't hear him.

She looked out of the window. How pathetic the garden looked as a result of the storm. There were so many flowers beaten to the ground. Deep runnels were carved into the soft muddy soil. The trees were bent, some of the branches broken off, and the blue petals of the jacaranda flowers lined the ground. But, she reminded herself, the sun still shone!

Walking with the dogs, she found the track was deep in mud, but she hardly noticed it, for she had too much to think about. What was love? she asked herself. How could she love a man she didn't understand? Alex had so many different facets to his character. Like the night before when he had been so understanding, considerate and gentle. Yet at other times he could hurt her with his sarcastic patronage, his refusal to treat her as an adult. It was so odd how quickly his nature could change. One moment he could be kind and the next cruel.

She bent and picked up part of a root, tossing it in the air for the dogs to run after. This time, as she stopped, Jock the spaniel looked up at her and wagged his tail. For a moment the tears were near as she gratefully patted him. At least there was one thing; Jock was starting to accept her. It was just as Alex had promised: 'Give Jock time and he'll let you replace Uncle Ned in his old dog's heart.'

Jon caught her breath. The painful truth of understanding shot through her. Never, but never, could she hope to have a place in Alex's heart. She would always be, to him, Uncle Ned's *little Jon*. Never, but never, would he see her as a woman, capable of love.

Despite the dogs' reproachful looks, she turned back and slowly walked up the track towards the house. Suppose, just suppose, Alex was in love with her mother?

How, Jon asked herself, how could she endure it? Dancing at their wedding? Perhaps even sharing a home with them?

No . . . no . . . no . . . !

She found herself running, the dogs, all save

old Jock, were having a whale of a time, jumping round her, barking with glee. But Jon was not running for *glee*—she was trying to escape from the horror of the thought she'd had. The intolerable, unbearable horror—living under the same roof as Alex, loving him and knowing he saw her as a stepchild!

If that happened, Jon told herself, she would sell the farm. But not to Alex, because she knew that she could never forget Uncle Ned's letter and his last wish. If she was unhappy, she could sell the farm—but never to Alex.

Soon after breakfast Madeleine phoned.

'Are you all right, Jon?' she asked considerately. 'It was a nasty storm last night. I hope your mother wasn't too scared? I know how she hates storms.'

'She didn't seem to mind,' Jon said simply. Did Madeleine know that Alex had spent the night in the guest room? Had he told her?

'Did you have much damage done?'

'The garden looks rather pathetic,' Jon admitted. 'You are coming tonight, aren't you?' Madeleine asked.

Jon hesitated, for she had not seen her mother to ask her, but Alex had said she'd seemed pleased.

'Yes, thanks,' Jon said, and wondered how she could end the conversation.

After a seemingly endless period of time during which Jon waited expectantly for

Madeleine to tease her about being scared of storms and needing a man's shoulder to lean on, it came to an end and at last, sighing with relief, Jon could hang up.

Almost immediately the phone bell rang again. This time it was her mother.

'Darling, the river is going down, but they don't think it's going to be all right until much later, so don't expect me home until after tea. What time are we supposed to be at the Foxes'?'

'About seven, I think.'

'That's fine. It'll give me time to have a bath and change. We dress formally, I would imagine. I gather they're very wealthy people?'

Jon laughed, 'I honestly don't know, Mum, but I'll find out.'

'Good, darling. See you later. You are all right? It was quite a storm. I thought of you all alone in that isolated little house.'

Jon's mouth twisted wryly. 'I had the dogs, Mum.'

'I know, dear, but the lightning . . . Anyhow, see you later.'

Jon went and stood on the stoep. How quiet it was, she thought. The long day stretched ahead. After this rain, there would be no ploughing, that was for sure. She could hear distant chatter and laughter from the workers in the pineapple fields. She sat down. There was nothing to stop her from thinking . . . of Alex, of course. Who else?

She could hear the trees' leaves rustling in the gentle breeze and the chatter of the tiny brightly-coloured birds who hovered over each flower, thrusting deep long beaks in as they searched for pollen. It was amusing to hear the birds chattering. It was almost as if they were squabbling about their rights, perhaps accusing one bird of jumping the queue, and they were such lovely colours, gold, palest pink, some even green.

How could she have been so daft, she asked herself, as to fall in love with a man like Alex? How could she go on living here, seeing Alex every day, knowing she was a nuisance, that everyone was watching her, almost hungrily, to see how long she could last? Why did they want her to fail? Why did . . .

She sat up suddenly. She had forgotten about the advertisement she had put in the local newspaper. It would be published on Friday and . . .

Sudden hope rushed through her. Once she had a good farm manager, she could ignore and avoid Alex. She might even manage to go away for a few months and leave her mother and Alex to make up their minds about the future. Could Alex be in love with her mother? Or Mum with him? Mum was a young forty-one. No one believed she was as old as that. She was very attractive, too. And Alex was thirty-five, so there was very little difference between them.

Oh yes, Jon thought, suddenly remembering she had promised to find out about what clothes they should wear. She jumped up, hurried to the telephone.

A strange husky voice answered. 'Madeleine's out, I'm afraid. I imagine she's with Alex, trailing around after him. She usually is.' The deep husky voice paused as she laughed, 'That girl will never grow up! The best way to lose a man is to chase him. Can I give her a message?'

Jon felt uncomfortable as she listened. Who was this—speaking so nastily about Madeleine?

'I'm Jon Hampton,' she said. 'We've been invited to dinner and . . .'

'You're little Jon?' The husky voice sounded even more amused. 'I've been wanting to meet you. I hear so much about you. Yes, we're expecting you and your mother tonight. I'm Mrs Fox.'

'Madeleine's mother?'

There was another husky chuckle. 'No, her stepmother. I'm exactly two years older than Madeleine.'

'Oh!' Jon's face burned. 'I'm sorry, I didn't . . .'

Mrs Fox laughed. 'Don't be. How were you to know? Anyhow, once we meet, you'll know you could never have made that mistake when you had seen me! Now, what was it you wanted to know? The time? About seven. We're not a

107

very punctual family, I'm afraid.'

'I . . . we . . . Well, we're new here as you know, Mrs Fox,' said Jon, feeling and sounding awkward. 'Is it formal? I mean, do we . . .'

'Dress up?' Mrs Fox chuckled. 'Depends on how you feel. Sometimes I wear jeans, other times a long gown. Madeleine will be dressed up, you can be sure of that, if Alex is coming. Dear sweet Alex!' Mrs Fox chuckled. 'Have you fallen in love with him, too?'

Jon's face was bright red. How she wished she'd never phoned Madeleine's home! She managed a laugh.

'I suppose he is attractive, if you like that sort of rugged ugliness.'

Mrs Fox's laughter rang out. 'How lovely! You're so right—rugged ugliness, that describes Alex perfectly. I gather you left your heart behind on England's gloomy cold shores?'

Jon clutched at the unexpected straw. 'Yes, I did.'

Mrs Fox chuckled. 'Maybe it's just as well. Wherever Alex goes, he leaves a trail of broken hearts. I think he enjoys it, likes to see how many of us he can hurt.' Her voice was bitter. 'Well, little Jon, we'll see you tonight? Good. Goodbye.'

Jon replaced the receiver with a sigh of relief. But she knew one thing. She had no desire to go to Pumula that night, or any other night. Alex would be there, too.

Could she look at him? talk to him? receive with dignity his teasing? Could she do all this without betraying the truth?

She went out on to the stoep. It was still quiet. The lovely mountains in the distance were bright with but few shadows, for the sky was blue, with few clouds, and the sun hot. How beautiful it . . .

Suddenly she wanted to cry. She stood very still, biting her lower lip, clenching her hands, fighting the desire to weep. If her mother saw her with red eyes . . . worse still, if Alex did!

'Why, Uncle Ned, when you gave me such a lovely gift, has everything to go wrong?' she asked silently. 'I ought to be the happiest girl in the world, and instead I'm so miserable. I feel caught, I want to get away, right away, back to my safe little world with an interesting job and . . .'

She walked up and down the stoep restlessly. Even though the blue mountains of Kabuta were not *hers*, as Alex had sarcastically pointed out, the view of them was, and that should be enough.

Just look at the garden—despite the night of destruction. Look at that beautiful tree, the trunk so straight, almost arrogantly so, with branches growing out at equal angles, as if designed by some famous architect. Everything was so lovely—the large green lawn, the frangipanis with their pretty pink fragrant flowers, the cannas with their gay yellows and reds, the huge dark red dahlias, their buds just opened. It was all so lovely and it was all hers, given to her by Uncle Ned who had loved Jabula and known she would love it, too. Was she going to give up all this simply because she loved a man who saw her as a girl of fourteen? Other people had broken hearts and survived. Why couldn't she?

She drew a long deep breath. No, she would not sell the farm. Somehow she would find a really good farm manager and . . .

'I'll give you a penny for them,' a deep familiar voice said. Jon swung round, startled to see Alex in the doorway to the house.

'I didn't hear you come in,' she said almost accusingly.

'I came in through the back. Your *induna* sent me a message as one of the tractors is giving trouble. By the way, I asked Violet to make us some coffee. Okay?'

'Of course.' She sat down. 'Sit . . .' she began, but Alex had already done so, stretching out his long legs as he smiled at her.

'Sleep well?'

She nodded, clenching her hands, trying to keep her voice even, to avoid looking directly at him. 'Yes, thanks to you. It was good of you, Alex.'

He laughed, 'Simply self-preservation. It saved me from getting wet on the way home. Did you hear me leave?'

Her mouth was suddenly dry. So he had

stayed with a selfish motive? Not to protect her, to give her a feeling of confidence in the storm because she had a companion, as she had thought.

'No,' she said curtly.

The coffee came and Alex poured it out. 'Sugar?' he asked casually, and she knew a moment of swift anger. What right had he to act in this house as if it was his home? Then she thought again. He and Uncle Ned had been so close, and he had looked on Uncle Ned as a father.

But it was never going to be his real home. As Uncle Ned wished . . .

She glanced at her wrist and her thoughts skidded to a standstill as she saw the small red thing, stuck in her skin just above her wrist.

It could only be a tick—and Madeleine had warned her about them.

'Look!' Jon held out her arm in dismay and Alex was on his feet instantly, taking her arm in his hand.

'Panic over,' he said as he deftly removed the tick and turned away with it.

Jon was shocked to find herself trembling. 'Madeleine said I . . . I must pull the tick out slowly, making sure the head came, or it would . . . I mean the sore would turn septic and . . . and goodness knows what else.'

Alex turned and sat down. 'Look, Jon, take everything Madeleine says with a pinch of salt. She'll twist anything. Not that I blame her.

111

She's had ten years of what must be hell, ever since her mother died and her father remarried. Incidentally, and before I forget it, Jon, put vaseline on a tick if you're unhappy about pulling it out, then the tick will drop off in time.'

Jon shuddered. Much as she loved this country, there were things in it that made her feel sick, just as there must be in every country of the world. Here it was the incessant war with the mosquitoes and now the ticks . . . She shivered. Alex's head was turned away as he drank his coffee and it gave her a chance to study each line of that rugged face, the small flat ears, the dimple in his chin, the way his hair was rumpled.

Alex turned his head suddenly and caught her staring at him. Her cheeks were hot as she braced herself for his sarcastic comment. Why was she trembling? she wondered. Was it the fright the tick had given her? Or that strange electric feeling that had shot through her when he took her arm in his hand?

'When do you expect your mother home?' Alex asked.

The unexpected question, so different from what she had feared, jerked Jon back to her usual self-control.

'After tea.'

'Not until then?' He sounded disappointed, she thought, then he stood up. 'I must be off, but Jon, would you come up to the sanctuary this afternoon? I've got visitors coming and I'd like you to play hostess. Besides, you've never been round the sanctuary and I'd like you to see it.' He laughed. 'Don't look so scared, little Jon. All you'll have to do is pour out the tea. See you about three? Okay?'

She was puzzled. Why ask her when Madeleine was so handy? Maybe she had something else to do?

'I . . .' She began, groping for a logical excuse, but Alex smiled at her.

It was a new kind of smile, a different sort of smile, a smile that made her want to throw her arms round his neck.

'Thanks, Jon,' he said gently. 'I knew you wouldn't let me down.'

And then he was gone. She stood very still as she stared after him. How could she bear it? To be so near him and yet so far away.

*   *   *

Jon dressed carefully that afternoon in a simple cream-coloured sheath frock. Her dark hair was brushed back from her high forehead and her eyes were wary though, as she drove through Alex's sanctuary, she kept telling herself there was nothing to worry about *that* afternoon. Alex would be too busy with his visitors to watch her critically. As he had said, all she had to do was pour out the tea!

It was to turn out very differently. As she

113

drove slowly along his winding earth road, she kept getting glimpses of monkeys swinging from the trees, a young giraffe running with his strange loping gait, an ostrich who stood in the middle of the road, blocking Jon's way and staring at the car with suspicion for a long time before, in the end, she turned away with disdain and Jon could drive on. As she came in sight of the house, a cloud of pale blue little birds flew up from the track in front of her.

She had parked the car when Alex came to meet her. How attractive he looked! His sun-bleached hair was still wet from a shower, his square face with the deep-set half-closed eyes and his square chin with the cleft in it that sometimes looked like a dimple. Oh, she thought, unhappiness flooding her, if only she didn't love him so much!

'Good girl,' he said, looking her up and down appraisingly. 'Perfect. I like a woman to look like a woman. Feminine! I also like her to be punctual, methodical and neat.'

She was not sure if he was joking or serious, but somehow she found courage enough to make a joke of it.

'So for once I'm a woman in your eyes, Alex? Quite a change from the impression I usually get.'

His eyes narrowed. You look like a woman today, but are you one? You are so young and naïve.'

'I'm twenty-three . . .' she began, and made

a big effort so that she could laugh. 'I'm afraid I'll have to send to Somerset House for a copy of my birth certificate, because you'll never believe me.'

He laughed, 'I'm not calling you a liar, little Jon. You're like your mother. She looks so absurdly young, too.'

The depression flooded Jon again. Back to her mother!

Alex glanced at his watch. 'My visitors are late. Let's sit down and have a cold drink. Right?'

It was pleasant on the long attractive stoep with its view of the valley below. But it could have been infinitely more pleasant, Jon knew, if she had felt less tense, less scared of what might lie ahead, less wary and watchful of her reactions to his teasing, less afraid lest she reveal her secret.

Fortunately Alex talked most of the time, telling her of his dislike of pineapple and indeed, any kind of farming.

'I never was a farmer at heart. Originally I was a game warden, and I loved that life. Then my parents died and left me the farm. They'd worked hard on it and I felt I owed it to them to make a go of it, but it was no good. In the end, your uncle told me I was wasting time, energy and my money. He helped me begin the sanctuary.'

Jon listened, entranced, and, without realizing it, she became more and more relaxed as Alex told her funny stories of how he had caught the wild animals, and how often things went wrong. And then, quite suddenly, the pleasant relaxed atmosphere vanished as he said: 'I'm ambitious, but I need more land.'

There was an uncomfortable silence as Jon's body stiffened and she concentrated on looking at her hands so that she could avoid looking at Alex. Why had Uncle Ned been so emphatic? she wondered. Why mustn't she ever sell the farm to Alex? Her uncle must have had a reason. If only she knew what it was!

At that moment, fortunately, three huge cars drove up and Alex led Jon to greet them. There were about ten people, most of them friendly Americans, eager to see everything, talking of the great beauty of this beautiful land, and looking at Jon with unasked questions in their eyes.

It was a perfect afternoon, hot but with a pleasant breeze so that the animals had not hidden themselves deep in the undergrowth. Alex, with Jon by his side, introduced them to his beautiful wild birds with their long stalk-like legs and their lovely pink wings and long beaks. They saw the giraffes, the baboons, the monkeys, too. Afterwards Jon poured out tea, though most asked for coffee which Alex's Jeremiah instantly produced. Finally after a round of talking and laughter the visitors left and Alex walked with Jon to her car.

'Thanks for lending me a hand. This may help a lot. Two or three of them write for magazines in the States and say they'll get me some publicity. They certainly had some super cameras.'

'Thanks for a pleasant afternoon,' Jon said, and meant it, for she had enjoyed it all, except for that awkward moment when Alex had said he needed more land.

Her mother was at home.

'I was getting worried, wondering where you were, Jon. Couldn't you have left a note?'

'I'm sorry, Mum, I never thought of it. Actually I didn't think I'd be away so long. Alex didn't . . .'

'Alex?' Her mother turned round quickly, frowning a little. 'You've been with Alex?'

'Yes, he had some visitors and wanted a hostess.'

Her mother laughed. 'Of course, that's right. He told me about it the other day and asked me to stand in. Was it very boring?'

'No. I . . . I quite enjoyed it.'

'I'm so glad, for you seem to have such a dull life here. Alex told me Madeleine had other plans for this afternoon and so he asked me. I suppose when I wasn't available, he was glad to have you.'

'Yes,' Jon said, her voice dull.

That was all she was to Alex—a stand-in, someone you can make use of or totally ignore, a nuisance because she needed help, a

117

pest because she refused to sell him the farm he wanted.

'By the way, Mum,' Jon went on, 'I rang the Foxes. We can dress or not as we like.'

'I'll have a bath now, then. I had such a lovely time,' Ursula said, and Jon watched her slowly stretch her arms and thought for the millionth time perhaps that she wished she was as lovely as her mother. 'It's a pity you don't mix well, darling, they're such nice people, but not the kind you like. My bridge is improving, the Colonel says.'

'The Colonel?'

'Yes, Colonel Harding. He lives near Qwaleni—a widower, and most charming. Perfect manners.' Her mother wrinkled her nose and in some incredible way, Jon thought, succeeded in looking even more beautiful than before. 'If only he wasn't so old!'

'Old?'

Her mother laughed. 'Old in your eyes, darling, for he must be well over fifty. I confess I prefer younger men,' she said, and went to the bathroom.

Jon stood still, gazing without seeing them at the blue mountains. Was her mother in love with Alex? And he with her? If only she knew!

But if she did know, she asked herself, would that help? Wouldn't it make it harder still to bear?

The phone rang—their party number and Alex's voice.

'Is your mother back?'

His voice was so curt, as to a schoolgirl, that Jon found it hard to answer casually: 'Yes, she's having a bath.'

'Oh, I see. Look, Jon, I'll fetch you tonight at six-forty-five. Okay?'

'I can drive us . . .' Jon began, but he brushed her words aside.

'You don't know the way and we may be home late. No one knows what can happen at Pumula,' he said, and rang off.

How right he was Jon was to find out about two hours later as in Alex's car they drove up the mountainside and over the top. Dusk was falling, but the clouded sky was still bright with the red of sunset. They drove past the highwire fence of the sanctuary and along the rutted earth road until at last they drove through open wrought iron gates, vaguely reminiscent of an old English manor house's entrance, and along a narrow lane with trees either side whose leafed branches met overhead and formed a long green tunnel. Finally they came to the house. Jon stared at it, startled. It was a three-storied house, tall, narrow, stretching up into the sky. Each floor had a verandah running right round the building. The roof was of tiles, the curtains of each window drawn.

'What a peculiar house!' said Ursula.

Alex laughed. 'We call it Cox's Folly. Apparently Samuel Fox's mother was an eccentric but a very wealthy one, too. She had plenty of protégés, young writers, artists and finally an architect. She wanted to help him, but he was a proud young man, so she decided to get him to design a house for her. This was it. We think he was joking, never expecting she would accept it. But she did, and there you are. The most unsuitable sort of house for this climate, of course.'

As he spoke the front door opened and a girl with red hair stood there. She wore a trouser suit of green silk and every movement she made was graceful as she came out.

'Alex darling, long time no see!' she teased the tall man who smiled back politely but with a coldness that startled Jon. 'Mrs Hampton and little Jon!'

'Ursula . . . this is Caroline Fox. Jon . . .'

Caroline smiled, 'I'm delighted to meet you, Mrs Hampton. I see how right the local gossip is. You must have been barely out of the cradle and little Jon . . .' Now Caroline Fox turned to Jon, a strange smile on her face, almost a triumphant smile, Jon thought uneasily. 'You must be the bravest girl in the world. Few of us dare antagonize our darling Alex.' She smiled at him. 'But I would add a word of warning, little Jon. It's well known that Alex always gets what he wants, no matter what it costs. Usually the cost is a broken heart. Not his, of course. But I forgot, you left your heart in England, didn't you?'

Jon coloured. She heard the startled gasp

from her mother, who stared at her and said: 'Jon, you couldn't be serious? Not Jimmy?' Her voice was full of contempt, and suddenly Jon was angry. It was her business whom she loved, and poor Jimmy hadn't been so bad, just unutterably boring.

'What's wrong with Jimmy? He's rather a darling.'

'But . . .' her mother began, but Caroline Fox ushered them into the house which was as strange inside as it was out. The whole of the ground floor was, apparently, one large lofty room, almost packed with chairs and couches, each one covered with a different but bright colour, such as crimson, yellow, white, or even a deep purple.

'Madeleine, where are your manners?' Caroline cried sharply, and Madeleine appeared in the gallery that circled the room and came down the curved staircase. She was wearing a long blue silk frock, exquisitely embroidered with a low neckline.

'Hullo. I didn't hear the bell,' she said, and as she spoke, a door above banged open and four small boys came tumbling out, racing down the stairs, almost falling over, nearly pushing Madeleine down. They were in pale blue shortie pyjamas, their heads wet. They had obviously been born eighteen months apart.

Caroline laughed, 'My offspring, Mrs Hampton. The eldest is Derrick, the next is

Donald, then Daniel and then Dennis. The four little D's.' She laughed again, 'How right that is, the little devils!'

The boys were racing round the hall, shouting at one another, jumping on and off the chairs, bumping into the visitors, screaming as one fell on the ground, landing on his nose. Caroline ignored them, and led the way through the big room to a small mosquito-screened patio at the back.

'Please see to the drinks, Alex,' she said. 'Samuel overslept and is still showering.'

They all sat down in the cane chairs and Caroline and Ursula Hampton discussed the bad storm of the night before while Jon and Madeleine sat in an awkward silence. Jon felt uncomfortably aware that she must look as if she hadn't bothered to 'dress'. Madeleine's frock was lovely, her stepmother's green silk trouser suit the essence of elegance, Jon's mother was wearing an old gold silk gown that was long and slinky, but Jon had merely worn her kaftan. Now, as occasionally Caroline's critical eyes drifted to look at Jon, Jon felt uneasy.

Alex was handing round drinks, and as he gave Jon her glass, a tall thin man in his late forties, came down the staircase. Jon stared at him, fascinated, for he was so handsome, it just wasn't true. He was more like a film star than any man she had ever seen. As he apologized and stood by his wife, he ran his hand lightly down her arm and when she smiled up at him, he smiled back. It was the sort of smile Jon would like Alex to smile at *her*, she knew.

Samuel Fox proved to be a delightful host, telling funny anecdotes, encouraging conversation, able to listen with apparent interest as well. Despite this Jon felt acutely uncomfortable. For two reasons: the first the closeness of Alex and the need for being on guard lest she reveal her love, and secondly, Madeleine.

It wasn't that her father and stepmother were actually *cruel* to her, it was much more subtle, such as when Madeleine's father said the boys should be in bed.

'You should have had them there long ago,' he said, his voice gently disapproving. But Jon saw the quick hurt in Madeleine's eyes as she went off to gather the four protesting little boys, who shouted and yelled and kicked her.

'Little devils, aren't they?' Caroline said with a smile. 'She just spoils them.'

Later Madeleine had been talking to Jon when Caroline said sharply, 'Don't sit on the nuts, Madeleine dear. Pass Alex some. You're forgetting our guests, but it's not like you to forget *him*.'

Nothing much, perhaps, some might call them little pinpricks, but each one hurt Madeleine, Jon saw with amazement. Jon was seeing a totally different Madeleine from the patronizing Madeleine she knew, and she also

123

saw the way Madeleine looked at Alex and a surprisingly warm wave of sympathy went through her, and for the first time she understood what Alex had meant what he said he was sorry for Madeleine.

Obviously she had adored her father, and then he had married a beautiful young girl, only two years older than his own daughter, whom he obviously loved dearly and who had given him four sons and taken the place in his heart not only of Madeleine's real mother but herself, too.

Though Madeleine could have left, Jon thought, instead of staying here to be criticized, made use of, and given the inferiority complex Alex had spoken of . . . for the situation must, at times, be almost unbearable. Then Jon saw the aching miserable look on Madeleine's face as she stared at Alex and Jon understood.

The time passed and they didn't eat and Jon wondered what time they would go home. Not that it mattered, for her mother was thoroughly enjoying herself, laughing a lot, her beauty renewed by her vivaciousness as she joked with the two men and Caroline. Actually it was the two youngest of the party, Jon and Madeleine, who were the quiet ones, occasionally chatting but more often silently listening. Jon also noticed the way Madeleine watched Alex, particularly when he talked to Ursula Hampton. Was Madeleine thinking the same as herself? Jon wondered.

They ate at last and it was a delicious dinner. Soup, thick mushroom soup; then duckling, tender and tasty, followed by a chocolate soufflé.

It was midnight before Alex led the way to his car, flashing his torch, his hand under Ursula Hampton's elbow. Jon walked behind them and was suddenly aware that Alex was talking quietly to her mother, so quietly that it was obvious he did not wish Jon to hear what he was saying.

A sudden irresistible urge made Jon move forward swiftly and quietly, and she just heard the words:

'. . . eight o'clock.'

She stood still, letting them draw away from her, and then followed them.

The journey was quiet and it wasn't until Jon was in bed that she realized what Alex's words must have meant. 'Eight o'clock' was the time Jon was usually walking with the dogs, for they generally had breakfast at eight-thirty! So Alex must have arranged for a time when Jon would be out of the way.

Jon buried her face in the pillow and the tears came. She knew one thing. That morning she would see to it that it was very late when she got home for breakfast!

*   *   *

Jon walked farther than she had ever done before the next morning. In the night there had been a heavy fall of rain so the earth track was muddy and there was little pleasure in the walk. The dogs, of course, loved every moment of it, even the old spaniel showing his first signs of interest in chasing the birds out of the pineapple plants.

Jon kept glancing at her wrist watch, for Alex had said eight o'clock, so she mustn't get home until after half past eight at the earliest, and by then he would have gone. She had no desire to see him . . . if he didn't want to see her!

Why? Why? She asked herself again and again. Why had she to fall in love with Alex? It couldn't be a more difficult, impossible situation.

When she got back to the house, she hastily changed and went out on to the stoep with an apology for being late for breakfast ready, but as she stepped outside she stood still, startled, for the stoep was empty. There could only be one answer. Her mother had got tired of waiting for her breakfast and had it. Dorcas came running from the bedrooms, holding out a note to Jon. It was short.

'Darling, we waited for you, but Alex had to go to Qwaleni early. He's taking me in to do some shopping. I may not be back to lunch so don't worry. Love, Mother.'

We waited for you . . . Jon's mouth twisted

ruefully. Had they waited for her? Or had they been glad she was late as it gave them the excuse they wanted in order to go alone? But would Alex need an excuse? If he wanted to take her mother into Qwaleni, he would simply say so. Jon knew he wouldn't think it was necessary to explain why he didn't want to take her as well!

'Your breakfast . . .' Violet was saying worriedly.

'I'm not hungry. Just some coffee, please,' Jon said wearily, and sat down alone on the stoep.

She felt a sense of desolation. Let's face it, she told herself, you were hoping hard that when you got back, Alex would still be here. Yet, at the same time, you dread meeting him in case he sees how much you love him. What sort of nightmare existence is it going to be for you—living like this? Why not sell the farm? Not to Alex, of course, for that would be going against Uncle Ned's wishes, but to someone else. Uncle Ned would understand, he always understood . . .

Then she could go away. Far, far away. Right across the world, perhaps. Too far to have to be at their wedding . . .

Suddenly she could bear it no more. She gulped down her coffee, jumped to her feet, calling the dogs and taking them for another long walk, as there was nothing else for her to do. That day they were spraying on the farm

127

and Alex would have told the *induna* what to do and what the men's jobs were to be. Dorcas and Violet kept the house spotless, so what was there for her to do?

Jon had walked far from the house, the dogs jumping into the shallow water of the irrigation stream, when she remembered something. On that day the local paper would come out and her advertisement be in it. That was the answer. Why did she keep forgetting that she had found the solution? Once she had a competent farm manager, she need no longer be dependent on Alex, no longer be a nuisance, or the laughing-stock of the neighbourhood.

She would show them! She was her uncle's niece, and she didn't give up so easily. Her footsteps were suddenly lighter, her shoulders back, she almost danced along the muddy track.

After lunch she would drive to the nearby store and get the local paper to make sure her advertisement was in it.

Later she drove down. She was careful not to open the paper eagerly in the store, for she knew there were curious eyes everywhere and that the small groups of farmers' wives would be quick to question her eagerness to read the local newspaper, and then, if they saw the advertisement, might put two and two together. She opened the newspaper as soon as she got home. Sitting in the car, quickly turning the pages, she saw that it was there

'Manager wanted for pineapple farm. Experience essential. Single man preferred. Write Box . . .'

'Hi! Suddenly interested in local politics?' a familiar voice asked.

Jon jumped, crumpling the paper as she looked up at Alex's amused face as he stood by the car. Of all people, he was the last . . .

'I wondered what was on at the Drive-In,' she improvised swiftly.

'You're on the wrong page.' Alex sounded amused.

'Oh, thanks.' Jon's hands were trembling a little as she dutifully opened the paper and searched for the Drive-In's advertisement. 'Mum was saying the other day she'd like to go.'

'We'll take her some time.' Alex opened the car door for her and stood back as she got out, clutching the newspaper tightly. 'How about some coffee?' he asked. 'I've only just got back from Qwaleni. Pity you weren't here, you could have come along.'

She walked ahead, careful not to look at him. Was that a lie? Had he been glad she was safely out of the way so that they could be alone?

'The girls are off duty this afternoon, so I'll make us some coffee. I expect Mum has put the kettle on,' she said over her shoulder, uncomfortably aware of the silence and afraid that he might ask to look at the paper.

'Your mum's not here.' Alex sounded as surprised as Jon looked as she turned to stare at him.

'I thought you took her to Qwaleni. She left me a note.'

'I did take her. She's having lunch with someone there—a Colonel someone or other. He phoned her while I was here and when she said she'd get you to drive her into Qwaleni, I said I could give her a lift, as I know how you hate that drive.'

'I see,' Jon said, but she didn't, not really.

She made coffee and they sat on the stoep, with long strange silences between them. She kept thinking of the advertisement, wondering if she should tell Alex and ask his advice, since she knew so little, had no idea what sort of salary she should offer a manager or if they had a contract or it was on a monthly basis. She decided to ask him careful questions and crossed her fingers so that she would give nothing away.

'An awful lot of farms down here are run by managers, aren't they?' she said casually. 'The Peters are managing a farm for some people in Hairadi.'

'Quite usual,' Alex said, lighting a cigarette slowly. 'A lot of business men invest their money in these farms but haven't a clue how to run them, so they employ farm managers.'

'It can't be much fun managing someone

130

else's farm,' Jon said thoughtfully.

Alex looked amused. 'It has its advantages. If there's a bad drought and the harvest is a failure, your boss bears the financial burden, not you.'

'But you'd feel just as bad! After all those months of hard work . . .'

'Farming is a gamble, little Jon. That has to be accepted. You can go up, up, up—or down, down, down. No matter how hard you work, at the last moment, nature can ruin everything. There's nothing you can do about it.'

'Do they get paid well? The managers, I mean?'

'Sometimes yes, sometimes no. Often not well, but they get perks—free house, electricity, use of transport and a bonus if it's a good year.'

Jon drew a deep breath. 'What do you call well?'

'Well? Let's see . . .' Much to Jon's relief, Alex gave her a good idea of the average salary of a farm manager.

'Do they have to sign a contract?'

He shrugged. 'Sometimes yes and sometimes no. Usually it's on a monthly basis.' He stood up. 'Thanks for the coffee. I'll just go round and see how the spraying is getting on.'

'Thanks.' Jon stood up, suddenly uncomfortable. 'Alex, you've been so good. I'm sorry I'm such a nuisance, but . . .'

She was about to tell him the truth—that

131

she had advertised for a farm manager and that soon he would be relieved of his irksome 'duties'.

Alex frowned. 'Who the hell ever said you were a nuisance?' he asked, his voice angry. 'I promised your uncle I'd help you.' Suddenly his hands were on her shoulders as he looked, down at her. 'Little Jon,' he said severely, 'how many times must I tell you not to believe everything Madeleine says? You saw for yourself the life she leads. I expect you wondered why she doesn't leave home?'

Trying to stand still, conscious of his fingers pressing into her flesh, she looked up at him. No, she didn't wonder. She knew why Madeleine stayed in her unhappy home. It was because she loved Alex.

She nodded, wishing yet again that he would stop calling her *little Jon*.

'Two reasons,' Alex went on. 'One, she loves her little stepbrothers. They adore her and she them. Two: she's bone lazy. Fond as I am of the girl, Jon, let's face it, she just hasn't got the guts to go out into the world and keep herself. Her father is a fine man but old-fashioned. If Madeleine left home—except to get married, of course—he might feel she had let him down badly, and he wouldn't help her financially. She's never been trained to work. How could she earn enough to keep her in the way in which she's accustomed?' he chanted the words, laughing, and releasing Jon.

Jon took a step back. Suddenly she felt very much alone—desolate, which was a strange thing, for Alex was still standing there, looking down at her.

'You're very fond of Madeleine, aren't you?' she said, and was then appalled at what she had said. She felt her face slowly burning as she saw the amusement in Alex's eyes.

'Yes, I am fond of Madeleine,' he said slowly, turning away. He paused by the steps down to the garden and looked at her again. 'Unfortunately—or so she says—I'm not the marrying kind.'

Jon stared at him. 'Won't you ever marry?' she almost whispered. What about . . .? she was thinking.

Alex laughed. 'Who knows? One day I may meet someone.' He shrugged his shoulders. 'I might ask *you* that question. Is it true you left your heart in England?' He was laughing at her, she knew that.

'Not my heart,' she said slowly, 'but my affection.'

She blushed painfully as he flung back his head and laughed.

'Honestly, little Jon, you slay me at times. What book are you reading? *Wuthering Heights*?'

She stood very still after he had gone, repeating the words over and over again: 'Not my heart but my affection.'

It did sound old-fashioned, stiff, even corny,

yet it was the truth and she had tried to cling to the truth. She had been fond of Jimmy, but she hadn't *loved* him. Never before had she loved anyone. She knew that now. She had never known what love was—what it meant. The joy and the pain; the desolation and delight, the futile hoping, the utter hopelessness of her love for Alex. If only . . .

CHAPTER SIX

It proved easier to get a manager for the farm than Jon had ever dared hope. Of course, she went through some bad moments, because she hated deceiving her mother, yet she knew that if she told her, Alex would have been told immediately and then he would probably insist on engaging the manager himself, and Jon wanted none of this. It was her farm and she intended choosing her own manager.

She had four replies to the advertisement, but only one was a single man. The other three were married and with children. This constituted a real difficulty, as the guest house would take some time to repair and repaint, so she replied to the single man, Tim Dean, and eventually drove into Qwaleni to interview him. This, also, was difficult, as she had to arrange it so that she went alone! However, she managed it in the end and went to the interview a little scared as she had no idea what she should ask or say.

It turned out, however, to be a very pleasant meeting. She liked Tim Dean as soon as she met him. He was a tall, too thin man with a long, rather horse-like face, blond hair which was also long, almost to his shoulders. Maybe he reminded her of England and the gay clothes and long hair, for she liked his scarlet shorts and white and red striped shirt. Her first thought was of what Alex would say, and knowing that he would probably disapprove maybe also made her feel favourably towards Tim. She was feeling defiant and rebellious, for Alex had been more than usually patronizing lately, teasing her, insisting on calling her 'little Jon'.

Anyhow, meeting Tim gave her the pleasant feeling that at last she would be treated as an adult and with respect. Here was a man with whom she could laugh, completely at ease.

Tim was polite as he asked questions about the farm and she told him, briefly, of her inheritance, and of the help Alex Roe had been.

'However,' she said as they sat talking in the lounge of the George Hotel, 'I can't expect Mr Roe to go on helping me indefinitely, so I need a manager. You have had experience with pineapples?'

Tim Dean had grey eyes and a quick smile that lit up his whole face. 'I've had experience with everything, Miss Hampton. Name it and I've farmed it.' He smiled. 'I quite see why you want a manager, though. As you say, it's a bind if you're constantly in debt to another person.'

'You know Mr Roe?' Jon sipped her coffee after having tried to keep her voice steady as she spoke of Alex.

Tim grinned. 'I know of him, but have never met him.'

Jon was embarrassed, though, when they talked of salaries and seeing the dismay on Tim's face, she immediately raised her offer. Then she told him that later there would be a guest cottage he could have, but at the moment he could eat with them but have his own bedsitting-room.

'But you must feel free to come and go as you like,' she said hastily.

'Sounds fine to me, Miss Hampton. When shall I start?' Then he laughed, 'I should say, *if* you decide to engage me, that is.'

Jon relaxed happily. This was the solution to all her problems.

'And I would say *if* you'd like the job.'

How nice it was to be treated as an adult, she was thinking. Never once had he suggested that she was too young. She asked him his age and learned that he was twenty-seven. Of course she said nothing, but she thought he looked much younger.

Now Tim held out his hand. 'It's a bargain. I think we'll make a very good team. Shall I move in on Sunday and start work on Monday?'

Jon smiled happily. 'That'll be perfect.'

She drove home, singing despite the heat of the sun. Her troubles were over. She was independent. She had her own manager. No longer would Alex have to come over every day, no more need he waste his precious time helping her, now he could devote all his time to his sanctuary.

The rest of the week seemed to drag by and Jon found herself trying again and again to tell her mother that on Sunday they were getting a permanent 'visitor'. It was odd, but now that she had definitely engaged Tim Dean, it was harder than before to word the news.

How would her mother react? she often wondered. Would she see it as an insult to Alex? She might even say she wanted no stranger in the house. Actually, of course, it was nothing to do with her mother, she reassured herself, for the farm was hers, and the money.

Not that she had many opportunities to talk to her mother these days, for Ursula now had so many friends that she was nearly always out. However, when Sunday came at last, the rain teemed down and the roads were bad, so Jon's mother decided not to go to church and that they would have a fire, for it could be bitterly cold when it rained so heavily.

Meanwhile Jon had quietly arranged the

137

guest room, telling Dorcas to make the bed, moving an armchair and small table in, wondering a little why her mother had not noticed or said anything. But then, Jon thought, these days her mother rarely noticed *anything*!

Now, just after the midday meal as they sat by the fire with the rain sliding down the windows noisily, she knew the moment had come. She could wait no longer, for Tim Dean might turn up at any time and if her mother didn't know . . .

'Mum . . .' she began.

Her mother was watching the flames jumping up round the huge log in the fireplace and she didn't answer.

'Mummy!' Jon said more loudly, and her mother turned her head.

'Yes?' she said, her voice dreamy.

Jon stared at her. These days her mother seemed to live in a dream world. True, it was for the best as there were far fewer complaints, but she was always looking as if her thoughts were far away. All the same, her dreams made her look even lovelier than ever, Jon thought.

'Mum, are you happier here?' she asked, surprising herself as much as her mother.

'Am I happier?' Ursula seemed to be thinking for a moment and then her face brightened with a smile. 'Yes, darling, I think I am. Why?'

'I . . . well, I just wondered.' Jon slid down

on the rug by the fire. The dogs were on the stoep for they were covered with mud. She glanced at her watch, wondering when Tim Dean would arrive. 'Mum,' she went on, 'I've engaged a manager for the farm.'

'Have you, darling?' Her mother yawned. 'This fire is lovely, but it makes one sleepy.'

'Yes.' Jon turned round, kneeling, looking up at her mother, puzzled by the calm acceptance of her statement. 'He's coming today and is going to live in the guest room until we've got the guest cottage repaired.'

Her mother yawned again. 'What a good idea, darling. It will be nice having a man about the house at night. I shall sleep much better.'

'Mum . . .' Jon hesitated and then turned her back on her mother, curling up in front of the fire with the little cat and gazing at the flickering flames as she realized that her mother was so totally uninterested in the farm and its fate that she didn't even care if Jon had a manager or not! Worried as she had been about her mother's reaction, Jon was surprised to find that this indifference hurt her even more. She had been so sure her mother would have been *against* the idea, for earlier on, she had wanted Jon to *sell* the farm, and surely she must know that hiring a manager showed how determined Jon was to make a success of the farm and never to sell it? But she seemed to have lost all interest, either way.

There was the sound of a car followed by the mad barking of the dogs and Jon jumped to her feet, going to open the door.

It was Tim Dean. His car was a red Mini. Now he smiled, pulling out two heavy suitcases and walking up the steps.

'What a day,' he said cheerfully. 'Hope I'm not too early.'

'Of course not. Do come in. Leave your cases there and one of the girls can bring them in,' Jon said, successfully shooing the dogs back to the stoep again as she led the way indoors.

'It's all right, thanks, I can manage,' Tim said, coming in close behind her.

Her mother was obviously stifling a yawn, but she smiled:

'You must be our new manager.'

Tim put down the suitcase and held out his hand.

'Are you Miss Hampton's mother?' There was just the right amount of shocked, unbelieving surprise in his voice and Jon saw, by the way her mother's eyes sparkled, that she appreciated the unspoken compliment.

'You poor man,' she said. 'You're wet through.'

Tim laughed. 'I had a puncture and had to change the tyre in the rain, but I'm used to it.'

'We can't let you have pneumonia as soon as you arrive. Jon, run the bath for . . . for . . . ?'

'Tim Dean, but I hope you'll call me Tim,'

he said with a smile.

Ursula stood up. 'Of course, Tim. Run the bath, Jon, while I show Tim to his room. Afterwards we'll have some hot coffee waiting for you.'

'It's very kind of you.'

She smiled at him. 'Not at all, Tim.'

Jon went to the bathroom, put out towels, turned the taps, feeling immensely relieved. Tim was going to fit in all right. There had always been a little fear in her mind that her mother might not like Tim and that he might fail in some way. But instead her mother was obviously delighted.

Ursula sat down by the fire, yawning. 'He seems a nice lad,' she said sleepily.

'I'll get the coffee, Mum,' Jon offered.

'Thanks, darling,' her mother said, and yawned again.

But she woke up when Tim joined them. He was wearing a red velvet smoking jacket and narrow white trews. His long hair was wet and curling on the nape of his neck.

'This is good,' he said as he sipped the coffee.

They were laughing and talking by the fire when another car drew up. Before Jon could stand up, she heard the car door slam, the footsteps of someone on the stoep and the front door opened.

Alex stood in the doorway. He was drenched. His clothes wet and clinging to him.

'I came to tell you . . .' he began, then stopped as he saw Tim Dean.

Jon's mother spoke quickly: 'I want you to meet Tim Dean, our new manager, Alex.'

Jon's heart seemed to skip a beat as Alex looked at her, his eyes narrowing. 'Tim Dean? I don't think we've met.'

Tim Dean had stood up. Now he smiled and held out his hand.

'No, sir, but I've heard of you.'

Jon saw that Alex's mouth was a thin line as he turned to her.

'I have to speak to you alone.'

'Come into the dining-room. Excuse us . . .' she mumbled, embarrassed, her legs stiff. It had been a mistake, a terrible mistake. She knew that now, even before Alex spoke. She should have asked his advice!

He closed the door and stood leaning against it as he looked at her.

'What's all this nonsense?'

She drew a long deep breath, lifted her head and looked up at him. 'It isn't nonsense. I've engaged Tim Dean to manage the farm.'

Alex folded his arms, his eyebrows almost meeting as he frowned.

'And what experience have you had in engaging farm managers?'

'It's my farm and my money,' Jon said, grateful for the anger that was flooding her because of his arrogant manner, for it gave her courage.

142

'Your uncle told you to ask my advice. You knew that. Why didn't you tell me you wanted a farm manager? I'd have got you a good one.'

She was startled. 'You would have?'

'For crying out loud!' He sounded more exasperated and weary than angry now. 'Grow up, Jon. I've been helping you all this time and I don't begrudge a moment of it, but if you'd said you'd prefer a manager, I'd have got you a good . . .'

'You don't know Mr Dean. He may be a very good one . . .' Jon began angrily.

Alex smiled, and Jon found it far more infuriating than if he had lost his temper again. 'Right, you've asked for it, Jon. We'll just wait and see what happens.'

He opened the door and then turned as if remembering something.

'I came to tell you that the road to Somahaha is under water. Have you enough food for a few days? If not, let me know. I've a deep-freeze that's packed full.'

He led the way back to the lounge and Ursula Hampton said quickly: 'Why, Alex, you're as wet as poor Tim was! How about a quick bath and we'll dry your clothes . . .'

He smiled. 'No, thanks all the same. I just wanted to tell you the road to Somahaha is under water.' He glanced at Tim Dean. 'How did you get through?'

'I didn't have to. I've been staying with the Oswalds.'

Jon saw the quick frown on Alex's face. She had only met the Oswalds once and liked them, but they were the talk of the dorp. Everyone called them 'hippies' because they wore brightly coloured clothes and his hair was long. The wife was a brilliant artist and the husband taught at a local school.

'You were lucky,' Alex said grimly. 'Your car'd never have got through.'

'What happened, sir?' Tim asked.

Alex frowned. 'The small dam overflowed.'

'Aren't they going to build . . .' Tim began, but Alex had turned to Jon.

'Don't forget, little Jon, that if you need me or any food, just give me a ring.'

'But you'll come and see us?' Ursula sounded dismayed. 'And can't I go out at all? I mean . . .'

Alex laughed. 'You can come and see me, the Coxes and down to the Oswalds.' His mouth twisted wryly. 'Take your choice, Ursula.'

Tim Dean stepped forward. 'I understood from . . . from Miss Hampton that you've been helping her with the farm, sir. I would appreciate it if you'd advise me, too, for the first few days.'

'I thought you were an experienced farmer,' Alex said curtly.

Tim smiled. 'I hope I am, sir, but you must admit that every farm has its own methods and I'd hate to unwittingly undo the good you've done.'

Alex went on frowning for a moment and then smiled. 'I see your point. I'll be here at four-thirty tomorrow.'

Jon saw the dismay on Tim's face which he promptly hid with a quick smile. 'That's very good of you, sir.'

Alex's mouth was a thin line as Jon went outside on the stoep with him, closing the housedoor behind her. 'I'm sorry, Alex,' she said quietly.

He turned and looked down at her, his eyes narrowed.

'Just what are you apologizing for?' he asked coldly.

'Well, I . . . I think perhaps I should have asked your advice first and . . .'

He shrugged. 'It's too late now. We must just wait and see how it works out. He may be all right.' He shrugged his shoulders again and then frowned. 'Just one thing, little Jon. Tell him to cut out the *sir* business, will you?'

'He's only being polite.'

'Polite my . . .' Again Alex's mouth was a thin hard line. 'Look, anyone would think I was his grandfather. How old is he, anyhow?'

'Twenty-seven.' Suddenly Jon wanted to laugh—so even hard, arrogant Alex was human where age was concerned!

'That makes me eight years his senior, so let's cut out the *sir* business. Will you tell him or shall I?'

145

'I will,' she said quickly, and then looked up at the man by her side. 'I don't want you to misunderstand me, Alex,' she said earnestly. 'I just didn't like being a nuisance to you.'

He was not smiling as he replied: 'I think you're more likely to be a nuisance now than you were before,' he said curtly, then ran down through the rain to his car.

She watched him reverse and drive away. Then she still stood on the stoep, her hands on the wet rail, herself unconscious of the rain that fell on her hair and shoulders, for all she could think of was how she had hurt Alex by her behaviour. Why hadn't she realized that Alex would help her find a good manager? But then again, wasn't Alex rather jumping to conclusions? How did he know Tim might not prove to be the perfect farm manager? Was it Tim's longish hair and his gay clothes?

'Jon!' her mother called impatiently. 'You'll get wet through!'

The door opened and Tim stood there, an odd smile on his face. 'I'm afraid I didn't make a very good impression,' he said wistfully.

She knew a moment of deep sympathy for him. Had Alex the same effect on others as he had on her? 'You don't need to worry. Alex's bark is worse than his bite. Only drop the *sir* business, Tim. It made him feel like an old man.'

'Well, he must be nearly forty. I thought he'd like me to be respectful,' Tim began.

146

Jon had to laugh. 'Forty isn't old, you know, not really. My mother's forty-one,' she added softly. 'So don't ever dare to say that or you'll break her heart.'

He smiled, 'Don't worry, I won't. I'm not that sort of a fool.'

*　　　*　　　*

Jon slept badly that night. She had been a long time falling asleep, for she went over and over again the scene when Alex had arrived. To her, it had become enormously important that Tim Dean should make a good impression on Alex, but would he? This was what was worrying her.

She could not forget the dismayed look on Tim's face when Alex had said he'd be there at four-thirty next day! At the same time, Tim was not a child and surely he could be trusted not to let her down on this, his first day?

Yet there were some people who just could not get up early. Some who openly admitted that they were only half awake until midday. Alex now was obviously the reverse. He seemed to thrive on early rising.

Now as she woke up, she stroked Rex's ears, trying to reassure as well as comfort herself. What did it really matter if Tim *was* asleep when Alex came round? It was no business of Alex's if Tim overslept. Of course it was no business, but, she thought with a shiver despite the heat that was already coming, what a

147

weapon Alex would have!

She lay still, looking out of the window at the magical colour of the sky as the sun began to rise. How lovely everything was here! Dear Uncle Ned, how right he'd been, guessing that she would love it just as much as he did.

Reluctantly, for she was trying not to start worrying again, she glanced at her watch. Four-fifteen. She sat up and Rex followed suit, looking at her expectantly and then, with an almost human sigh, he lay down again as he saw she had no intention of getting out of bed. Instead she propped herself up with pillows and watched the slow but relentless movement of the second hand of her watch.

How long would it take to dress? Was he one of those men who bath every morning? If he kept Alex waiting . . . would Alex wait? The impatient shrilling of an alarm clock reassured her. She relaxed, but the whining angry noise went on and on and she sat up again. Tim must be a heavy sleeper not to hear that noise.

She was half out of bed before she stopped herself, shocked by her impulsive movement, for she had been about to rush along the passage and bang on Tim's door. How could she do that? What on earth would he think? Probably be furious with her. Making her appear like a nagging wife . . . !

Suddenly the shrill cry of the alarm stopped and Jon sighed with relief. In a short time she heard the cranky sound of the shower in the bathroom and she lay down under the thin sheet that was all the cover she needed these hot nights. All would be well, she told herself, and drifted off into a deep sleep.

She awoke at her usual time and hastily pulled on jeans and a shirt and took the dogs for their morning walk before the heat of the sun was too great. Later on, the humidity would make it almost impossible, for they were going through a spell of storms with cold rain followed by days of intense heat.

How quiet the house was, she thought, as they went out of the kitchen door. No sign of Alex's car or horse, no sound of voices. So obviously everything was all right.

Despite the thick mud of the track, her spirits lifted. No longer need she worry about Alex's reactions. Tim would take over, cope with everything. He would teach her about farming so that one day she could manage alone. That was her ambition—or her determination, perhaps, was the better word. She had to prove to Alex that she was not a naïve helpless child but a woman, able to cope with any problems that could arise.

And not only must she convince Alex but all the people of the neighbourhood who were laughing at her behind her back and waiting with such cruel maliciousness for her to fail.

She skipped a little with joy. She would show them! Yes . . .

She tripped over a big stone and fell

149

headlong in the mud. For a moment she lay still, then scrambled to her feet, looking at her mud-covered jeans and hands.

'Well, well!' an amused and all too familiar voice said, 'I'm not accustomed to such worship, my little Jon. It really wasn't necessary to grovel in the mud at my feet. What's wrong this time?'

She glared at Alex. 'I wish you wouldn't always creep up on me as you do!'

'Are you out of your mind?' Alex sounded even more amused. 'I was following you up, but you were dancing along like a young impala. Why are you so happy? Your new manager?'

Jon had forgotten Tim, but now she wondered how that first meeting had gone. She tried to look calm and at ease as she studied Alex's rugged face. 'You came this morning?'

'I said I would, didn't I?'

It was not a question, more of a reminder that he always kept his word.

'Well?' she asked.

'Well?' he asked in turn with a smile.

They stared at one another, each silent as if completely oblivious to the beauty of the mountains and not noticing the dogs as they chased one another. Jon felt breathless, but she clung to her self-control, digging her long nails into the palms of her hands, welcoming the pain as her composure slipped away. If only he would stop looking at her like that!

'Well, what did you think of Tim?' she managed to say.

'It's difficult to judge after such a brief meeting, but I'd say he knows his job.'

A wave of relief swept through her. She had expected a sarcastic answer. 'You think he'll be all right?'

Alex shrugged. 'Who can tell? Only time. Anyhow, Jon, you know you can phone me if any problem arises that Dean can't cope with. I'm not far away. Be seeing you!' He turned and walked rapidly away.

Jon still stood where she was, unable to move. So that was that! Alex had washed his hands of her for good.

That was what he obviously meant. Of course, she could phone him. How very nice! Very thoughtful! What would Uncle Ned say? she wondered. Alex was supposed to help her, not just walk out at the first opportunity. Madeleine was right, then. Alex had found Jabula and its inhabitants nothing but a nuisance, a burden he had now gladly shrugged off.

She stopped her thoughts abruptly, shocked by her bitterness and injustice. It was her own fault, entirely. This was what she wanted and she had made it plain enough, surely? Alex had quietly and with dignity accepted the situation.

And yet she was blaming him for doing just

what she had wanted him to do! How unutterably stupid can you be? she asked herself.

Now as dark grey clouds had suddenly appeared, massing up so that they hid the mountains, Jon walked back slowly to the house. She heard her mother's voice as the dogs raced ahead. Was Alex still there?

Jon went to the back door and the bathroom for a quick shower and then put on a clean pink frock. She went slowly to the stoep. But it wasn't Alex there, it was Tim, looking clean and spruce in a pale fawn safari suit and making her mother's eyes shine with interest.

Breakfast was a gay meal on the surface, but deep inside her, Jon could not forget the look in Alex's eyes and then the casualness of his voice as he said curtly: 'Be seeing you!' and walked off.

She loved that man, she thought miserably. How she loved him! Why was she behaving like Madeleine? Staying and suffering. Wouldn't it be better to sell the farm and go far, far away? Canada, or even Australia— anywhere that she could live without the risk of meeting him. Just suppose he learned the truth—that she loved him so? How he would laugh at her! She could imagine him saying: 'Is our little Jon growing up at last?' and her cheeks would burn and her temper boil over and she would say something terrible and . . .

'Excuse me,' she mumbled, and stood up, hurrying to the safety of the bathroom where she could stand for a moment, pressing her hands against her eyes, fighting the tears that were so near.

She bathed her eyes in cold water, scolding herself, for if her mother noticed the tears, she might mention them to Alex and . . .

But would her mother notice? Jon asked herself. These days her mother seemed to be living in another world of her own. Jon was glad for her mother's sake as well as her own, but sometimes she missed the loving fussiness her mother had practised in the days when they lived in Bexhill. Today, she felt, her mother rarely *saw* her at all.

When Jon went back to the breakfast table, she saw that she hadn't even been missed! Her mother was saying: 'Yes, I'd love to go to the Drive-In, Tim. We must get a local paper and see what's on.'

'I know,' Tim said with a grin. 'I've seen the film, but it's worth seeing a dozen times.'

'What's it called?' Jon asked, not because she was really interested but because she wanted to appear as if she was behaving normally.

Tim grinned. 'A good title. *What Is This Thing Called Love?*'

Jon caught her breath and with another unnoticed murmur slipped from the room again. She heard her mother say: 'Is it an A or

153

an X film?'

Tim was laughing. 'It's very subtle. You'd enjoy it.'

Jon closed the bathroom door and leant against it. 'What is this thing called love?' she repeated slowly. She had always thought love would mean happiness. Maybe it did if you fell in love with the right man. A man who could love you, could see you as a woman and not as a child, the niece of his best friend.

If only . . .

What was it Alex was always saying?' You'll get used to it.' Would she? Would she ever get over this desolate heartache, the feeling of hopelessness, the pain?

'Jon . . . Jon darling!' her mother called

Jon hurriedly returned, hoping her mother would not ask her why she'd left the room, but Ursula was laughing:

'Jon, Tim's taking me to the Drive-In tonight. Like to come?'

'I don't . . .' Jon began, but Tim was on his feet.

'Of course she'll come. The more she learns about love the better. We're at the dangerous age, aren't we, Jon?'

'Are we?' She managed to smile.

Next day when Jon drove down to the store to shop, she was alone, as her mother had decided not to come, as though they had heard the water was down, it was far too high for her liking.

There was a sudden hush as Jon walked into the large building and she wondered if they had been talking about her. Then as she got the basket and walked round the closely-packed shelves, looking at her shopping list and pretending not to notice the way the people were looking at her, the voices and laughter began again.

No one spoke to her until she went to pay and then a group of women who had been talking greeted her.

'Hullo, Jon, how are things? Is it true that you've got a manager?' asked one.

'I thought Alex managed everything for you,' said another.

'We all thought you'd sell the farm,' a third butted in.

Jon faced them all. There was nothing malicious, she knew, in their gossip. In a small group of people where nothing much happens the smallest bit of gossip becomes fascinating.

'Alex has been helping me,' Jon said calmly, 'but I can't expect him to do it all the time, because he has his own work.'

A burly man in grey shorts and a thin white shirt climbed down from a truck and came in, grinning at Jon. 'I hear you've got a hippie running your farm,' he teased.

She flushed. How people liked to use that word as an insult! What was wrong with being a hippie, after all?

'Is his hair really down to his waist?' old

Cliff went on. Jon knew him well; he often came to buy pineapples. Now he grinned at her, his blue eyes innocent of malice as he enjoyed a chance to bait her.

The laughing-stock of the neighbourhood, Madeleine had said, Jon remembered. Keeping her face solemn, she said: 'Actually, you know, his hair reaches to the ground.'

She heard the quick gasp of shock from someone near her, but old Cliff roared with laughter. 'I bet that makes Alex mad, because he'll be bald in a few years.' He calmed down and spoke more seriously. 'Look, Jon, is it going to work out?'

'I see no reason why it shouldn't,' Jon said rather stiffly, then regretted her tone, so she smiled: 'We always have Alex to give us advice.'

'Alex knows him?' Cliff sounded surprised. 'If Alex says he's okay then okay he is. I heard he'd been living with the Oswalds.'

'Staying with them,' Jon corrected him gently, then she felt her quick temper rising. 'And just what is wrong with the Oswalds?' she asked.

Old Cliff chuckled. 'You ask 'em, m'dear, not me. Anyway I'll be along your way later on, so I'll look in and have a peep. Hair down to the ground, bless me soul . . .' he was muttering, still chuckling as he went back to the truck. He had done no shopping at all, Jon noticed, so that meant he had recognized her car and come in simply to find out about the new manager!

As Jon paid her bill, the pretty young woman behind the desk smiled: 'I expect your ma will be glad to have a man about the house. You're a bit isolated there.'

Jon smiled. 'We are compared with where we lived before—right on the front at Bexhill in England.'

'But you're happy here?'

Jon drew a long deep breath. 'I'm very happy here,' she said, and as she drove home, she wondered if it was the truth. Yes, she was happy, she decided, except where Alex came into the picture. She liked the local people's friendliness. And nowhere could there have been nicer people than those who had opened their doors to her mother. Their friendliness had made her mother happy.

Driving along the avenue of jacarandas, she wished they might bloom for ever for all too soon, the bluebell-blue blossoms fell to the ground, leaving a carpet of colour.

Back home she was surprised to find her mother had gone out after all. 'Mrs Sellars came and said there was nothing to worry about the dam. I'm having a bridge lesson this afternoon, but will be back tonight as Tim is taking us out,' said the note.

Jon sighed. Tim and her mother seemed to have boundless energy. The night before they had gone to the Drive-In, getting home late. It was odd, but she got more tired doing nothing than when she worked so hard. Sometimes it worried her to think she was not using her qualities as a pharmacist. Was she right, trained as she was, in a world where so many people were ill, in leading this lazy life of leisure? One thing, when the winter came and the cooler days she was going to work on the garden. At the moment, it was far too hot.

She heard the sound of a horse and hurried out to the stoep, but it was only Madeleine. She left her horse to browse and despite the sun, ran across to the house. She wore elegantly cut green cotton trews, a white shirt, and her long blonde hair was brushed back, tied with a green ribbon.

'Hi, Jon!'

'Hi,' Jon replied stiffly.

Madeleine gazed at Tim's car. 'So it is true?'

'So what's true?' Jon asked, refusing to help. Then she saw the perspiration running down Madeleine's cheeks and thought of the times the girl had helped her, and felt a worm. 'Come inside,' she said. 'Like a cold drink?'

'With plenty of ice, please. It really is a scorcher. I think it's building up for another big storm.' Madeleine kicked off her shoes and stretched out on one of the chairs.

Jon took her time in the kitchen getting cold drinks and ice. Madeleine was reading the local paper when Jon joined her.

'Thanks. Cheers.'

'Cheers,' said Jon, looking across the beautifully cut lawn and thinking what a good job Robert had made of it. He was the garden-boy and a hard worker.

The mountains were shrouded in a dark mist and that part of the sky was hidden in low clouds.

'What's he like?' Madeleine asked with a yawn.

'What's who like?' Jon said stubbornly.

Madeleine laughed. 'Come off your high horse, Jon. Everyone's talking about it. You've got yourself a bachelor manager . . . "with a view to marriage should both parties prove suitable",' she quoted.

Jon coloured. 'I don't know what you're talking about.'

Madeleine laughed again. 'You're very touchy today, Jon. What's gone wrong? Are you missing Alex's constant visits? I was quoting the adverts you see in the paper for the Lonely Ladies column. You're looking for a husband to run the farm for you so you employ a handsome young bachelor. Simple. I'm glad that, at long last, you've admitted the truth.'

Jon was battling to control her temper. 'What truth?'

'The truth about Alex. He was really fed up, you know, running your farm plus his own work.'

'He said he didn't mind.'

'Of course he said that, he's too polite to tell the truth. Besides, he was crazy about your uncle.'

Jon sipped her cold drink slowly, looking at Madeleine thoughtfully. How different she was when away from her own home! It was difficult to believe that this aggressive, rude girl was the same meek girl at home who almost trembled if her father looked disapproving.

'Where's your mother?' Madeleine asked abruptly. 'She seems very popular these days.'

'She's made a lot of friends.'

'It's hard to realize she's over forty.'

'Only just. I hope I look as young as she does when I'm forty-one.'

'You probably will, seeing that you look about fifteen now,' Madeleine said bitterly. 'What's this new man like? I hear he's been living with the crazy Oswalds.'

'Am I intruding?' Tim opened the door to join them. He looked curiously at Madeleine, his thin horse-like face amused.

'Of course not, Tim,' said Jon, and introduced him. He sprawled in a chair.

'I'm bushed, Jon darling,' he said casually. 'Be an angel and get me a cold drink.'

'Sure,' Jon said, knowing how hot it could be out on the lands. As she went off to the kitchen, she wondered why he had called her darling. He never had before, but then it was a word casually used by theatrical and what Alex might call 'arty-crafty' people!

When she joined them again, Madeleine and Tim were joking like old friends, but they welcomed her, including her in the conversation.

'Now tell me, Tim,' said Madeleine, 'about the Oswalds. Why aren't they accepted here? I mean, you hear the queerest kind of rumours, all about orgies and black magic and things like that.'

Tim laughed. 'They lead busy lives and like to keep to themselves, so they make up half of the stories. You see, they're not athletic types, bored by cricket, hate sitting in a club drinking, so they don't want to mix. Although Mark is teaching, he is also working on his thesis—he's a great guy and will go a long way . . .'

'So will you, Dean,' a cold angry voice interrupted.

Startled, they turned round as Alex came out from the house. His legs and body were covered with dust, his face brown and stickily dirty, his hair thick with dust, too.

'There was an accident with one of the tractors at Mlutilon and they couldn't get you on the phone, Dean, so they called me. We had a job getting the man out from underneath. The tractor had gone down a slope. You can imagine the mess!'

Alex made an expressive gesture, showing his dirt.

'You can see the state I'm in doing your job,' he went on curtly. 'I'm taking Lucas straight to hospital, Jon, but you'd better go out, Dean, at once as the others need some first aid. Maybe you'd better go, too, Jon.'

Madeleine jumped to her feet, 'I'll go with Tim, Alex. I'm used to this sort of thing.'

Tim was on his feet. 'How did the accident happen?'

Alex's face was as cold as stone. 'Inefficient brakes. Lucas said he'd told you.'

'Lucas is a liar. We'll take the truck, Maddy,' Tim said, and they both hurried away.

Jon sat very still. She felt almost an intruder—at any rate completely inefficient. No one seemed to realize that as a pharmacist, she knew a lot about first aid. Maybe she should have said so, but it would only have started an argument and another chance for Alex to be sarcastic.

Alex, too, had gone, hurrying out to the waiting truck. Standing up, Jon could see the body of Lucas lying in the back of the truck with another African bending over him.

Jon caught her breath. What exactly had happened to Lucas? Would he be all right? It was a long bumpy road to the nearest hospital.

Inefficient brakes? Tim had answered that Lucas was a liar. But Lucas was one of their best drivers, young, alert, eager to learn and thoroughly reliable, Alex had said once. Yet it could be true. Lucas must have forgotten to tell Tim and to save himself from getting into trouble might have lied to Alex. In any case, if

162

Lucas had to be rushed to hospital, was he able to talk sensibly?

Jon wandered round the house miserably, thinking of how hot poor Lucas must be feeling, how the jerk of the truck must hurt any broken limb. She also felt horribly useless and lonely.

The girls had finished cleaning and were now in their rooms, chattering, laughing and listening to their radio. At twelve they would come back and get lunch. And now she had a farm manager . . .

Well, she told herself suddenly, self-pity won't get you anywhere. Do something constructive about it. So she showered and changed into a clean yellow frock, combed her hair back and went out to the car, leaving the dogs to look at her with reproachful eyes.

Jon was wondering why her mother had never learned to drive. It would have given her far more freedom, here.

'I'd much prefer to be driven,' Ursula always said when it was suggested. 'It's much more fun.'

Driving along the dusty road, battling with the tiny fruit flies that seemed to find the hot inside of a car inviting, Jon gave herself a scolding. She told herself she was ungrateful, stupid, despicable; that the average girl would be thrilled if she had been left such an exciting, beautiful heritage. How could anyone be so miserable when she had so much?

How angry Alex had been with Tim. But rightly so in a way, for it was Tim's job. How had it happened that Tim had not got the message? The clerk was usually in the office, and if Tim was out on the lands, supervising the work, the clerk should know where to find him.

It was funny, Jon thought with a sigh, how much more complicated life had become since she came to Africa to live. All the same, she loved it. Maybe Alex was right and you get used to things, she thought, as she realized that the winding climbing road she usually hated had not worried her at all.

She jammed on her brakes suddenly as a cow wandered out from behind a bush and began to cross the road. It was followed by more cattle, all strolling, looking aloof from the waiting car as if too proud to take notice of it. Then a small boy with a thin bit of skin tied round his middle came running out, waving a tiny stick. He looked at Jon and gave her a big grin and she waved to him as he hustled the cattle out of the way and watched with wide-open eyes as she drove by.

One of the hazards of driving, she reminded herself. Wasn't Alex always giving her lectures on the subject?

She was usually annoyed. 'I drove for four years in England.'

And he would look scornful. 'England is very different from Africa.'

He was right, too. She was glad he hadn't been there to see the way she had jammed on her brakes. She should have been watching for the cattle, because this was a particularly bad part.

In Qwaleni, she parked her car and went to the bookshop, not quite sure why she had come in or what she was looking for. She wandered round, looking at the shelves.

'Just what are you looking for?' a familiar voice asked.

Jon jumped, turning to find herself uncomfortably near Alex. He had obviously showered somewhere, for he was clean, though his safari suit was crumpled and dusty.

'How is Lucas?' she asked quickly.

'Going to be all right. Concussion, broken arm, two broken ribs. In hospital, of course. Good thing I was around.'

'Oh, it was. I can't think why the clerk wasn't in his office.'

'He was,' Alex said sternly. 'Dean was out and the clerk didn't know where. I'll tell young Dean that in future he must tell the clerk where he is.' His voice changed. 'However, these things happen at times. What are you looking for?'

'I thought I'd brush up my first aid as no one seems to think I know any.'

'Because I let Madeleine go with Dean?' Alex's voice became hard. 'Did you want to go with him?'

165

'Lucas is my employee, not Madeleine's.'

Suddenly Alex was smiling. 'Look, Jon, be sensible. Madeleine has lived out here since she was a child. She grew up here. She's used to accidents and coping with such problems. Imagine her in a lab. or a chemist's shop—she'd be lost, and you'd be at ease, confident you knew your job. You can't know everything. However, I have got a good book about first aid in the bush if you'd like it.'

'I would. I do want to be . . .' She stopped abruptly, for she had nearly said too much. She wanted to be part of the farm, able to take her rightful place as owner of it, and how could she be while she was still so ignorant? Yet if she said that to Alex, maybe his mood would change and he would start teasing her about what a rooinek could do and how little she knew. So she drew a long breath and began again: 'I'd like to learn their language, too. I mean, Violet and Dorcas are good at English and I feel . . . well . . .'

Alex smiled. 'Inferior because they can speak your language but you can't speak theirs. Well, let's face it, you haven't been here very long. However, it's an estimable idea.' He leant towards a shelf and pulled out a paperback book. 'This might help you.'

'Thanks.' Jon hastily looked through the pages and saw with dismay that it was going to be far from easy! But then neither was English easy, she reminded herself. 'I'll try.'

She looked up at him and saw that he was glancing through a book as if uninterested in what she was doing. Her heart ached as she looked at his rugged ugly-handsome face, his mouth that could be tender as well as cruel . . . If only she didn't love him so much!

Now he looked up. 'Well, what do you think of it?'

'It looks fine. I'll get Violet to help me.'

'I'm afraid I must go, as I've a lunch appointment.' He looked down at his suit ruefully. 'Well, they'll have to forgive me, that's all. See you!' he said cheerfully, and without giving her time to reply, walked away.

Suddenly the shop seemed cold and empty. As in a dream, Jon chose several magazines she knew her mother liked to read, and took them and the book to the counter to pay for them. She drove home more slowly, watching carefully for the cows or goats that might wander across the road.

The best thing for her to do was to be candid with Tim. She was sure he'd understand how important it was for her to know how to run the farm. It meant so much to her. So very much.

CHAPTER SEVEN

As the days became weeks, Tim became more and more a part of the Hampton family. It was so pleasant having him around, Jon thought happily, apart from the fact it had released her from depending so much upon Alex.

The house was full of laughter, her mother enjoyed his company, the farm ran smoothly, there were no more problems. Certainly Tim had changed many things, but either Alex did not know about them—which seemed unlikely, as he appeared to know everything—or he was uninterested or that it meant Tim was a success and Alex could not admit it.

Tim, for instance, never got up at four-thirty a.m. Instead he gave the *induna* directions the night before and left it to him to call the rota every morning. When Tim awoke and got up, he would take the truck and drive round, checking the work that was going on, but he always got back in time to accompany Jon on her early morning walks with the dogs. She enjoyed them, for he was full of amusing anecdotes and always ready to argue cheerfully with her when they failed to agree. With Tim, she was completely relaxed, not having to be on guard, watching her words. Yes, there was no doubt but that Tim was pleasant to have around, and having a farm manager had obviously been the right thing to do.

Of course, as she admitted privately to herself, there were a few disappointments, but then you could never have everything perfect. Tim, for instance, had not agreed when she asked him to take her round the farm with him, learning as she watched.

'Look, Jon,' he had said, his cheerful gaiety vanishing, his voice becoming almost stern, 'I can only be your manager if I'm left to handle it my way. I can't cope with my boss hanging on my tail all the time.'

'I wouldn't, Tim. I just . .' she had begun to explain, then had stopped, realizing that she couldn't tell him the truth: that she wanted to run the farm herself. That would mean that by teaching her, he would be preparing the way for his own dismissal.

Tim had changed as she paused, taking her hand in his. 'I do understand, Jon, you're bored to tears. After your life in England with an interesting job, this must be terrible. We'll go and see the Oswalds. Kirsty might be able to help you. She hated this life until she found out how to live here.'

'But I find farming interesting, don't you?' Jon had said.

Tim had smiled. 'Interesting? It's just a way of earning a living and it's darned hard work, too. Or can be, unless you're sane and know how to manage things. Take Alex Rose, for instance. Just a show-off. Getting up at four a.m. !' he had said scornfully. 'Anyone can run a farm this size without breaking his back.'

Then there had been the case of the little cat. One day she noticed the little cat had vanished. This was so unlike the little animal that Jon was worried, but before she had time to say anything—this was in the early days soon after Tim's arrival—Alex had arrived.

'I found your cat on my stoep. Goodness knows what made her come back to me,' he had said, holding out the small furry bundle.

'I'm so glad. I wondered where she was.' Jon had taken the cat into her arms and Tim, by her side, had sneezed violently.

'I didn't know this was your cat,' he said. 'I thought it was a stray. I'm allergic . . .' he sneezed again and again . . . 'to cats, I'm afraid.'

Jon, staring at him, had thought for one alarming moment that perhaps Tim had dumped the little cat somewhere, then she felt ashamed. Tim was not like that!

Alex had reacted instantly, taking the cat from her arms.

'I'll have him. He knows me well and I'm not allergic to anything,' he had said curtly.

Tim had been very upset and she had felt so sorry for him as he explained how embarrassing it was, sneezing all the time when a cat was around. She had remembered then that during his first days with them, he had sneezed a lot and her mother had thought he was getting a cold. However, she told herself happily, as she carefully weeded the seedlings she had planted in a carefully-built brick seed container, Kirsty Oswald had suggested it and Jon was getting a lot of pleasure from her new interest in gardening; there was no doubt that having Tim as a manager had been a wonderful idea. He was so amusing and interesting, too. When he was nineteen years old, he and a friend had set off round the world on what he called 'the thinnest shoestring ever'. His exploits were funny and Tim got many laughs when they went out to parties. A young attractive bachelor is always welcome in a small community and it seemed to be taken for granted that when Tim was asked out, Jon was included.

At first Jon had refused and she had seen Tim angry.

'Grow up, Jon. You don't want to get bush-happy.'

'Bush-happy? What's that?' she'd asked.

'It's when you live alone in the bush for too long, you get anti-people. You find it hard to talk to them, to make friends, and are apt to retreat into your shell of lonely misery and never leave it. You end up by being such a bore that no one wants to see you. Look, Jon, you're too young to fall into that trap, so you're coming along with me. Right?'

And she had realized that he was right. In

England, with her friends and work, she had been an extrovert. Here, with so little to do, she was fast becoming an introvert. She couldn't tell Tim, but she knew why! She still could not forget Madeleine telling her that she was the laughing-stock of the neighbourhood and that everyone was waiting for her to be sensible and sell the farm!

So Jon had gone out. Naturally they had to entertain, in return. Often her mother would be there, thoroughly enjoying herself, looking if anything younger than she had done when she first arrived, and obviously having forgotten her first fears and dislikes of the country! All this was largely because of Tim, Jon was thinking, as she deftly pulled out the tough weeds that threatened to suffocate the delicate seedlings.

The Oswalds, too, had helped a lot, she knew. Mark was tall, thin, with long blond hair. He usually wore khaki shorts and a vivid coloured shirt, usually open and showing the blond hairs on his chest. While teaching, he wore sandals. At home he went barefoot. He worked hard in the evenings and Jon found she could help him by going to the library and getting him the books he needed for research, or even writing away to the nearest city for them. Kirsty, his wife, rarely went out except to shop. Short, slender, she looked frail but was tough as nails, as Tim said. She wrote books but rarely sold them. When she did, they paid the family bills. Mostly she painted, and even introduced Jon into the fascination of oil painting.

So gradually Jon's empty days were becoming filled. Tim had even induced her to play tennis and now she was helping to cater for the Sunday lunches at the Club. This was all due to Tim, she knew, and she was grateful for it.

Christmas was coming closer and she found it hard to imagine a Christmas where the temperature could be in the hundred zone and the sun always shone. The thunderstorms of their earlier days seemed to have gone, but she knew they could return.

'If not rain, then hail,' someone had said. Jon had guessed he was teasing, for whoever heard of hail in the summer?

Jon straightened, looking proudly at the small healthy seedlings which would, she hoped, give colour to their garden. This was the wonderful part of this country: even in winter you had roses and sweet peas and all sorts of flowers. She wiped her brow and wondered if it was any cooler in Qwaleni, for her mother had been given a lift there by Alex.

Alex was still the biggest problem of her life, but she was learning to control herself and live with it. Sometimes she thought that he was in love with her mother—at other times she wondered if her mother appealed to Alex because she was so helpless and feminine,

173

which he obviously liked.

As she went into the house, it was terribly hot. Even the dogs had deserted her, hiding under the beds which were apparently the coolest spot at the moment. As before, Jon wondered what air-conditioning would cost. She had suggested it to her mother, but she had said it would be a waste of money if Jon finally decided to sell the farm.

Sell the farm? Never, Jon thought firmly, still irritated by people who kept asking her why she wouldn't. Uncle Ned had given her the farm and she was not going to sell it, she would say again and again.

'Hot, eh?' said Tim, coming out from his room. He had obviously been sleeping, for his hair was tousled, his face wet with sweat.

They sat on the stoep, leaving the doors open in the vain hope of getting a draught through as they drank long cold drinks. Suddenly she heard a terrible frightening roaring sound . . . She looked up and through the open door saw the small white plane, zooming so low over the trees that she felt sure it must hit one of the long branches—or even hit the house.

Somehow she must have stood up and turned impulsively, and she found herself in Tim's arms.

'It's all right,' he said, holding her close. 'It's only the plane spraying the plants.'

She began to laugh and cry at the same

time. 'How can I be so stupid . . .' she began, when Tim kissed her.

Startled, she drew away and he let her go. She stared at him.

'I'm sorry. It gave me such a fright—that dreadful noise . . .'

Tim smiled. 'Should I be sorry, too, for kissing you?'

For a moment she was dismayed. Why had he kissed her? Had she encouraged him? She liked him, but that was all . . .

Tim laughed, 'Don't look so scared, Jon. I've been waiting for a good chance. D'you know you're delicious, delightful and delectable?'

She could laugh, too, sharing the joke.

'Come and see the plane,' he said, leading her out on to the lawn. The plane came back. Once again Jon wondered how it could dare to zoom so low, but this time her fear was for the pilot, but as they watched the small bird-like plane climb up into the sky at a sharp angle, circling and returning, the pilot—easily seen in his small box-like part—waved. She waved back.

'Lucky guy,' Tim said enviously. 'He makes a fortune. Wish I could get such a job.'

'Have you tried?'

He nodded. 'Bad eyes.'

As they watched the small white plane glide, swoop and climb and then come back to zoom low over the fields, Tim explained about spraying.

To Jon, it was a fascinating experience, caught up in her imagination, she felt herself in the plane as it shuddered under her hands and she made it respond to her demands. How lovely it must be—high up in the beauty of the cloudless sky, leaving the earth with its problems far behind.

The plane landed on a distant runway. 'It's filling up. I want to see, so I'll go over. See you later.'

Jon hesitated. She would have liked to go, too, but she remembered Tim's strongly expressed determination not to be interfered with while on farm work, so she walked obediently back to the house.

She saw that the inside door to the house had been closed, and frowned. She was sure that both doors—the one outside and the house one—had been open when she and Tim were there. Maybe Violet had come to see her . . . or to take the empty glasses away. It never for a moment occurred to her that someone might have been standing there, witnessing the little scene in which she had stood in Tim's arms and he had kissed her. Reading into the scene, perhaps, everything that was not true.

CHAPTER EIGHT

Christmas came nearer, the shops were bright with decorations and, in some, the soft muted music of carols. Jon, who normally loved Christmas, found it hard to work up any enthusiasm.

She shopped, buying her mother a chiffon negligée and nightie and Tim a pipe, as he was always losing his and accusing the girls of having stolen it.

Surely there was no need to buy Alex a present? She rarely saw him these days except when he came to pick up her mother or they all met at a dinner party. As for Madeleine . . . well, no one could call them friends.

Tim brought home decorations and spent a hilarious evening putting them up.

'I'll bring up a Christmas tree at the last moment,' he promised.

'Isn't it rather a farce?' Jon said unhappily. 'We'll all be out.'

She could not forget the pain she had felt when her mother announced that she was going to spend Christmas with her friends. They had been sitting on the stoep in the early hours of the evening when the sky was streaked with crimson and green and the reddish sun slowly vanished behind the mountains. They were having their usual sundowner, when Ursula said:

'I don't know what your plans are for Christmas Day, Jon darling, but I've been invited to Qwaleni for the day with some friends.'

Jon could still remember the ridiculous hurt she had felt. Looking back, she could remember that in England, and ever since she was seventeen, she had refused invitation after invitation from friends who wanted her to spend Christmas with them. Her mother had known about these invitations and had accepted it as a fact that needed no discussing, for surely no loving daughter would dream of leaving her poor widowed mother alone!

Yet now her mother . . . this, their first Christmas in a strange land . . . Of course she wasn't a widow—but Jon could be lonely, too. Imagine a Christmas all alone!

Tim had leant forward. 'We've been asked to a braaivleis, Ursula, so don't worry about us.'

Later, much later, Jon had tackled Tim. 'It was good of you, but you don't have to, Tim. I mean, I know you made it up about that invitation.'

He grinned, 'But I didn't make it up. The Oswalds asked us, and I've been driving myself nearly silly to work out how we could leave your ma out. The Oswalds aren't her cup of tea, but I didn't want to upset her.'

'Is that the truth?' Jon asked worriedly. She

178

could not bear it if she spoiled Tim's Christmas for him.

He made a dramatic gesture. 'Cross my heart and all the rest. We'll have great fun, just the four of us. Mark's great at braaivleis and we can talk and talk and talk.'

So Jon had laughed and accepted the situation. But try as she might, she could not see her mother's side of it, and she had a vaguely unhappy feeling that her mother no longer loved her as she had before. Obviously her mother's friends were of a different age group. But they had been in England, too, yet her mother had loved the family Christmas, even though there were only two of them.

Suddenly she thought of something: Was it with Alex that her mother planned to spend Christmas?

It was a week before Christmas when Tim and Jon had been invited to the Oswalds for the evening. Jon's mother had already told them she was going out for the evening, but not who with. She rarely mentioned names these days, Jon thought miserably. There was no doubt about it, she and her mother were growing apart. Jon was in the bath when her mother called goodbye.

'Have a good time, Jon darling. I may be home late, so don't worry about me.'

Jon called goodbye and leisurely soaked in the refreshing bath. The Oswalds rarely dressed up, so she slipped on her red kaftan.

She loved the loose swinging sleeves, the comfortable feel of the silk material next to her skin.

As usual Tim was late, and Jon waited patiently. When he joined her, he was wearing a safari suit.

'Ready?' he asked impatiently, just as if she hadn't been already waiting for nearly an hour.

'We're late.'

'So what?' he grinned.

But when they got to the cottage the Oswalds were renting, they found a note pinned to the door.

'We waited as long as we could to tell you Mark has to go to Qwaleni about his job. We'll dine at the Prince Inn, so maybe see you there. Sorry and all that, Kirsty.'

Jon began to laugh. 'It must be important to drag Mark all that way.'

'Let's go to the Prince Inn, Jon. I've never been there.'

'Horribly expensive,' she warned him.

He grinned. 'Then let's go dutch, okay?'

'Okay.' Jon settled down by his side as the car shot off.

She was never very happy driving with Tim, for he not only drove fast but took chances. Once he had told her jokingly that he must have ninety-nine lives as there could be no other explanation for his continued survival.

Jon loathed back seat drivers herself, so she forced her hands to lie on her lap and kept her legs stiff so that her feet would not jam on imaginary brakes. She closed her eyes as the car jerked and swung round corners, bumped over corrugations, in and out of deep ruts. She must make herself think of something else . . .

Where was her mother dining that night? she wondered. It was strange how little she knew about Ursula's outings. Of course she didn't have to tell her, yet, in the past, she had seemed to delight in telling her everything, all she had done, and then would have asked Jon what *she* had done, too! Now she seemed quite uninterested. Jon tried to laugh at herself. Perhaps it meant that her mother now accepted the fact that her daughter was a woman and not a child! All the . . .

Jon stifled a startled sound as the car hit a bump, seemed to leap in the air, then landed with a bounce before roaring on.

Tim laughed, 'That was a close one. Stupid goat!'

'Did . . . did you hit him?'

'Course not. I'm not that daft. Why so quiet? Disappointed about the Oswalds?'

'Of course not. Just thinking.'

'About what?'

Jon clung to the side of the car as they went round a steep corner, swerving sideways. 'Life after death.'

Tim roared with laughter. 'Am I giving you the jivvies? Am I going too fast?'

'A . . . a bit.'

'Yellow, that's what you are. Chicken, Jon. All the best drivers in the world act crazy.'

Jon was wondering what Alex would have said when Tim shouted:

'Hold tight!'

The car plunged through a stream that meandered over the road, splashing up water so that the windscreen was nearly covered and Jon was splashed through the open window.

'They must have had rain earlier today, because that's new.' He sounded joyous. 'Bet that gave you a fright.'

'And how!' She could hardly speak as she wiped the muddy water off her face. 'Tim, I wonder if we're dressed enough for the Prince Inn? You haven't got a tie on.'

'Does that matter? Anyhow, let's give it a try.' He looked at her. 'We'll be off the earth in five minutes and then you can relax.'

'Good-oh.' She tried to laugh, but she felt a little shaken and sick. She wondered why, for she was not subject to car-sickness. She only hoped she was not getting the strange 'flu bug that seemed to be going round the district.

The tarred road was smooth and the jerking and swaying lessened though their speed increased, but at last they reached Qwaleni.

The Prince Inn was on the slope of a hill with a grand view over the valley where electric lights flickered and shone against the black background. There was even a moon to shine a swathe of light over the clusters of

182

trees and the narrow river that swerved past the houses. The Inn was modern and immensely popular, judging by the many parked cars.

They walked through the foyer towards the restaurant. The tables were grouped round the dance floor and a small band playing. Tim's hand was on her arm, his fingers pressing into her skin in time to the beat. 'Looks rather smart.'

Suddenly Jon stiffened. She couldn't believe it. Yet it was true. All her past fears were proving right.

Dancing on the floor was Alex. And in his arms, laughing up at him, was her mother!

Jon stopped dead so that Tim bumped into her. 'Steady on! What's wrong?'

'I . . . I feel sick . . .' Jon gasped, looking round for the cloakroom. I won't be a mo . . .' she muttered, and almost ran.

Alone, she stood still and gradually the nausea seemed to float away. She must surely be getting that 'flu bug, she told herself.

Had Alex seen her? And if he had, did it matter? But why all the secrecy? Why hadn't her mother said she was dining out with Alex? Why . . . why . . . ?

But she had no right to ask these questions, she knew. Her mother had the same right to live her own life without questions as Jon had often felt she had, when they lived in England.

Nor had she any right to feel hurt because

Alex had not asked her to join them. So often in the past, he had said:

'You don't mind a blind date, little Jon? I'm arranging a party', and she had refused, finding some stupid excuse. And why? Because she wanted no 'blind date' but to dance with Alex, and he had no desire to dance with her!

All the same, it was no wonder he had stopped inviting her out, was it?

She went back to the hall where Tim was sitting on a couch, a glass in his hand. He beckoned to her and she went and sat by him. It was a lofty hall with pillars and frescoes on the walls They were out of sight of the restaurant, so there was little danger of Alex seeing them.

'What happened?'

'I felt sick.'

'Come on suddenly?' he asked.

'I didn't feel too good in the car.'

He put his hand on hers. 'Silly girl,' he said gently. 'You should have told me. We needn't have come all this way.'

'I think it must be 'flu.'

'You don't want to dine here?'

She turned to him appealingly. 'No, please, Tim, no.' Her hand flew to her mouth. 'But the Oswalds are dining here.'

'They'd understand. It's very hot and noisy. We'll go to the Karrafin.'

When they went outside, there was a distant rumble and suddenly a vivid flash of fork lightning in the distance.

'Looks like a storm,' Jon said.

The Karrafin was much quieter and cooler. After a quick meal, Tim drove her home much more slowly. The rumbles of thunder were much closer, often crashing overhead as the great dark sky was rent with jagged flashes.

At home, the dogs welcomed them noisily.

'How about a cup of coffee?' Tim asked.

'I'll get it,' said Jon, letting the dogs out in the garden where they raced in circles, leaping in the air as they barked madly, but they soon came back to curl up at Jon's feet.

Jon had just finished her coffee when Tim said:

'Why do you hate Alex Roe so much?'

'H-hate him?'

'Yes. He was there tonight. That's what upset you. Why?'

'I don't hate him, but . . . but, well, he makes me mad. He will treat me as a child and he never stops teasing me. I hate sarcastic men, too.'

Tim grinned. 'Memo: Jon dislikes being teased. You never mind when I tease you.'

'That's different.' So very different, she thought, because I'm not in love with you. 'Alex seems to delight in making me feel small or humiliated.'

Tim had a strange expression on his face. 'Jon, it's tricky for me and that's why I've said nothing, because I thought you and your mum

185

were fond of Alex, so . . . Well, look, has he made you an offer for the farm, Jon? I heard a rumour, but . . .'

There was a startlingly white flash of lightning together with a terrific clap of thunder and then there was a dark silence.

Jon shivered, remembering how this had happened before, and how touched she had been by Alex's kindness only to discover that he had spent the night in the house to save himself from getting wet on the way home.

'Not an offer, but he does want the farm,' Jon said stiffly.

'Why? Does he give a reason?'

'He wants to enlarge his sanctuary, Tim.'

Tim grunted. 'That's a lie, make no mistake. Do you want the truth?'

'The truth?' Her voice was unsteady.

'Yes, the truth. Has he told you that they plan to build a dam and that, if so, this farm will be under water?'

Jon sat up, horrified. 'I didn't know. He didn't say. It can't be true! My farm?'

'Of course he didn't tell you, Jon. That would give the game away, wouldn't it? When the dam is built, you'll be given good compensation, a far higher sum than you'd get for the farm. That's why he wants to buy it. All he thinks of is money.'

'A dam . . .' she repeated slowly. Had Uncle Ned known? she wondered. Was that why he wouldn't sell it? But that didn't make sense, because he had told her in that secret letter that she could sell the farm, but not to Alex. Was it because he had found Alex trying to cheat him?

Alex? Cheating? She found it hard to believe.

'Alex isn't like that . . .' she began.

'That's what you think. How is it we're losing all our good labour? I didn't tell you, but more and more of them are walking out on us, and do you know why?'

Her mouth was dry. 'No.'

'Because Alex is paying them more than you can afford,' Tim said, almost triumphantly. 'He's sabotaging you, Jon. He's just determined to make you sell out to him.'

'That I never will!'

'He'll make you. He's utterly ruthless.' Tim stood up. 'Time for beddybyes.' He yawned and then looked down at her. 'Don't look so shocked. Alex is just a man. None of us are perfect.'

Lying in bed, Jon felt bewildered. Tim had seemed so sure that what he said was true. Some of it made sense. That could explain Uncle Ned's insistence that she must not sell to Alex. Yet how could she believe that Alex was planning to cheat her? How could you think that of the man you love?

Jon was asleep when her mother came home and when she awoke it was pouring with rain, so there was no walk for the dogs. She

187

stood with them on the stoep, looking at the rain as it pelted down from the grey cloud-massed sky, watching the water churn up the earth, drowning her precious seedlings, beating down the dahlias that were doing so well.

'What happened to you, last night, darling?' her mother said, startling her.

Jon swung round. 'What d'you mean?'

Her mother yawned. 'Alex saw you come into the restaurant and then you vanished. I thought you were going to the Oswalds. I'd told Alex so.'

'We were . . .' Jon was thinking quickly. What had Alex said? 'We were late getting there and they'd left us a message that Mark had to go to Qwaleni on business and if we liked, join them at the Prince Inn.'

'They were there. They joined the party.'

'The . . . the party?'

Her mother yawned again. 'It was great fun. Caroline and her husband, Madeleine and Alex, and we asked the Colonel, too. Alex wanted to ask you, but I knew you'd accepted the Oswalds' invitation, so I told him so.'

Jon stared at her mother. What a stupid idiot she had been, she told herself. But was it true? Or was her mother saying it to hide the fact that she had been alone with Alex? But if she had, did it matter? Why should her mother have to lie? It could only be the truth.

'Why didn't you come and join us when you

saw us, Jon? It was very rude. Alex seemed annoyed. What happened? He said you nearly fell over and that it was a good thing Tim had his arm round you, and then you vanished.'

Jon drew a deep breath. 'I felt ill. Tim drives fast and the road was rough and . . .'

'You poor darling. Where did you go?'

'It seemed so hot and noisy, so Tim took me to the Karrafin. It's cool and quieter.'

'I know. I often dine there with . . .'

Tim came up the steps, looking miserable, rain trickling down his face as he pulled off his thin yellow mackintosh.

'Hello. What a downpour! What time did you folks get home?'

'We didn't leave until nearly one and by then the worst of the storm was over.' The little bell rang. 'Good, breakfast. I'm hungry for once!'

Jon wasn't, but she managed to behave normally.

Halfway through the morning, Ursula was on the phone, talking, laughing, and Jon was alone on the stoep when she saw Alex, riding his big black horse. She stood up, meaning to escape, but he had seen her and lifted his hand in greeting.

He came up the steps, and she looked at him steadily. Was Tim right and could Alex be trying to cheat her? Maybe if she could make herself believe it, then she could stop loving him.

He kicked off his muddy boots. 'How are you feeling?' he asked. 'Your mother phoned to explain your extraordinary behaviour last night,' he said coldly.

'I thought I was getting the 'flu.'

'I see. You're sure it wasn't because you preferred to be alone with your manager?' The hint of sarcasm in his voice as he said the last word angered Jon immediately.

'We planned to meet the Oswalds there, but I felt ill. Tim thought it was too hot and noisy, so we . . .'

'Went to the Karrafin. A charming romantic little place. I trust you enjoyed yourselves,' he said, his sarcasm even more obvious.

'I . . . I felt ill,' she repeated.

Alex's rugged ugly-handsome face was grave.

'I suppose you do know what you're doing?'

'What I'm doing?' Jon was startled.

'You know very well what I mean. You may be naïve and young, but not as much as that! The local gossips are having a wonderful time. You realize that you're never seen without your bachelor manager? How long, they say, will he remain one?'

'One?'

Alex frowned. A bachelor.'

Suddenly she was angry again. 'Alex, I didn't think you listened to gossip. Or has Madeleine been talking? That was what she said at the beginning. She told me I had asked for a bachelor as I needed a husband. Well, I didn't and I don't . . .' She had to stop speaking because she was breathless.

'But does Tim know that? He calls you darling, putting his arm round you, and I've seen him kissing you.'

'Kissing me?' Jon began, then burst out laughing: 'Oh, that! The plane startled me and I fell in his arms.'

'How convenient for him—or should I say, for you?' Alex asked coldly.

'Alex, don't be absurd. He was only joking.'

'Since when was kissing a form of joking? It sounds very strange to me.'

'Alex, you're so square. You should have lived in the Victorian age. What's a kiss?'

He moved closer to her. 'If you don't know, it's time you did,' he said roughly, seizing her shoulders and jerking her towards him, leaning down and pressing his mouth hard against hers.

It was a kiss without love. A rough, cruel kiss, and yet . . . She jerked herself free.

'If that's what you call a kiss, I think it's hateful!' she said wildly, turning to the house door and almost stumbling through, but Alex's hand caught and held her still while she kept her face turned away.

'One other thing, little Jon,' he said angrily. 'Where the hell is your precious manager? The irrigation ditch is flooding, which means one of the drains is blocked. It's his job to clear them,

191

not mine, but if he doesn't get cracking soon, there may be big trouble.'

'He's . . . he's in the office,' Jon said, and his hand let go her arm. She shivered, missing the touch of his hot fingers, and then she was free, free to run to her bedroom, and to pass her mother who had just stopped phoning.

'Jon darling, is something wrong?' she asked.

'Just a headache,' Jon said, and escaped to her bedroom.

She stood very still after she had locked the door. She hadn't known what a real kiss was like before. But now she did!

CHAPTER NINE

Christmas came and Jon learned to laugh, to appear gay and hide the misery inside her. There were plenty of braaivleis and cocktail parties, and Tim insisted that she went to them all. He was always close by her side, his hand under her arm and always ready to take her home early if she asked him to.

Christmas Day came with the present-giving, and then a car came to fetch Jon's mother. Jon was rather surprised to see the elderly man with white hair, glasses and a friendly smile.

'Jon dear, this is Colonel Harding,' Ursula

said. 'He's teaching me bridge.'

'I have a good pupil,' he said with a smile.

'A good pupil depends on a good teacher. Have a lovely time, Jon darling,' Ursula said with a farewell kiss.

Jon found herself enjoying Christmas Day, as it was hot and they all went to the Club to swim in the pool. The two men went off to find beers and Kirsty and Jon lay in the sunshine, each seeking a tan colour. Kirsty's eyes were half-closed as she smiled at Jon.

'Are you serious about Tim?' she asked.

Jon was startled. 'Serious? No . . . I mean, I'm fond of him, but . . .'

'I think it's more than friendship on Tim's side,' Kirsty told her. 'Look, Jon, I like you, and though I'm fond of Tim, I'm not at all sure he's the right man for you. Please watch out. We hardly know him, really. Mark only met him just before Tim saw your advert. They had mutual friends in Canada, so we asked him to stay for the few days before he began working for you.'

Jon sat up and hugged her legs, her face worried. 'Kirsty, I hope you're wrong. I like Tim, but . . .'

'There's another man?' Kirsty's eyes were thoughtful. 'I see. A hopeless love?' She paused while Jon nodded and then sighed: 'You poor child! I went through all that when I was your age. It's part of growing up. I know it won't comfort you, but I can promise you that one day you will forget.'

'I only wish I could think that,' Jon said earnestly. 'But, Kirsty, I'm worried about Tim. Have I let him think . . . ?'

'Tim doesn't wait to be allowed to think. Just watch out, though, and don't fall for that little-boy-lost smile of his. Behind it lies a tough guy, selfish, ruthless . . .' She smiled at Jon's shocked face. 'He can't help it. He had a tough childhood. He's always had to fight for everything. I'm fond of him, but Jon, I wouldn't like to see you married to him.'

'I've no intention . . .' Jon began, and stopped, her face red, as two men joined them.

'No good intentions?' Mark teased as he lay down beside her. 'How different this is from an English Christmas, eh?'

'Very—very different,' Jon agreed, remembering the snow on the front at Bexhill, the waves coming racing in, roaring and splashing over the rail on to the pavement, their visit to church at midnight. But there had been another side to it, too, she reminded herself. Often they were asked out at Christmas, but preferred to stay home as her mother had a 'thing' about being pitied. So they would watch television to lessen the quietness.

'Very different, indeed,' Jon added.

Mark smiled, 'I hope this is nicer.'

'It's much more fun seeing the kids having such a wonderful time in the pool. Certainly

194

we know more people here. I can't imagine eating turkey and Christmas pudding with a temperature of nearly a hundred degrees Fahrenheit! I'm used to a cold Christmas.'

'You'll never go back to England?' Mark asked.

Jon shrugged. 'It depends on the farm.'

Tim smiled. 'You don't need to worry about that, Jon. That's my headache. We're doing fine.'

She smiled, 'I'm glad.'

As they drove home, Jon searched for the right words, but could not find them. How did you say: 'Look, I like you, but I can't marry you because I love someone else!'

After all, Tim had never said he loved her, never talked of marriage. His 'darlings' meant nothing—that was just Alex's old-fashioned notion. What should she do? Was she unmeaningly encouraging him? Yet what could she do about it? Refuse to go out with him? It wasn't as simple as that when Tim was living in the same house and working for her.

The Coxes, Madeleine's family, gave a New Year's Eve party. Everyone seemed to have been invited, but fortunately it was a beautiful night so they could sit outside on the lawn and stoep. Bright lights glowed, there were torches blazing to keep away the mosquitoes—and noise! The four small boys were racing around, shouting, screaming, while many of the local people were swimming in the pool.

Once again Jon was sorry for Madeleine. It was funny, she thought, that it was only in Madeleine's own home that she could ever like her! It was 'Madeleine, do this . . .' 'Madeleine, why haven't you done that? . . .' or even: 'Really, Madeleine, do you have to be so clumsy?' It must be an awful life, Jon thought sympathetically, as she watched poor Madeleine meekly doing what she was told, her eyes unhappy. Except when she danced with Alex, and then her face was radiant.

Was it the same with her? Jon worried anxiously. She only danced once with Alex. It was a strange dance, silent, and he held her away at a slight distance as if he had no desire to touch her. Yet all the same, she was in his arms . . . A small consolation, though, for when the music ended, Alex merely escorted her back to her chair, murmured a formal 'thank you' and walked off.

Jon's next partner was Madeleine's father and she thought again how amazingly handsome he was.

'If you do have to sell the farm,' he said casually, 'where would you go? Back to England?'

Jon looked up at him. 'I won't have to sell the farm.'

He smiled, a friendly smile. 'It's obvious you know very little about farming, my dear girl. There's always something—drought, hail, foot and mouth disease. There are thousands of hazards. Let's say, for the sake of argument, you had to sell.'

'Well, I don't know. I've always wanted to see the world. I might go to Canada or . . . or Australia.'

'You've enterprise, my dear. I wish Madeleine had. Sometimes I wonder why she stays with us, because it's no life for a young person. It's high time she got married and settled down. I just can't understand my daughter—the way she chases poor Alex. Has she no pride? I can't imagine you behaving like that.'

Jon blushed. 'It isn't easy to behave sensibly when you're in love.'

'Love!' Madeleine's father grunted as he made a neat turn. He was an excellent dancer, Jon thought. 'Love!' he repeated. 'That girl doesn't know what the word means.'

'She loves her brothers,' Jon said quietly, 'and you.'

'Think so? Sometimes I wonder. Caroline and I'd be much happier on our own, but you can't push your own daughter out when she doesn't want to go. Times I've offered to pay her return fare to go to London for a few months, but no, she can't leave her precious Alex. Personally I don't think she loves him— not one bit. What she wants is a wealthy husband. Alex is the wealthiest of us all. Did you know that?'

The music stopped, Jon smoothed down the

slightly creased skirt of her pale yellow silk frock. 'No, I didn't.'

'He keeps it quiet, but it's true. One of these days that man'll be a millionaire. You mark my words.'

There was a sudden quietness as the dancers dispersed to their seats and a clear voice broke the stillness.

'Alex, my darling!'

The words carried clearly and every head turned, including Jon's. In the doorway that led to the wide patio, a tall slim woman stood—pitch-black hair piled high on her head, what looked like a chain of diamonds twisted round it, sparkling in the light. She wore a long narrow scarlet sleeveless dress, reaching to the ground but slit at the sides so that as she moved forward, her long beautiful legs could be seen plainly. Her hands outstretched, she went straight to Alex.

'Darling . . . darling Alex!' she said loudly. She put her arms round his neck, rose on tiptoe and kissed him lovingly. 'It's been so long, love,' she went on as the startled silence continued.

'Too long?' Alex was asking, deftly unfolding her clinging arms. 'Whose fault was that?'

Jon turned her head and saw that Caroline, Madeleine's stepmother, was by her side. 'Who's that?' Jon whispered.

'Just another scalp our wonderful Alex has

198

to dangle from his belt,' Caroline said, her face and voice bitter. 'She's Antonia Herd, the film star. She's supposed to have broken her heart because Alex refused to leave his beloved sanctuary and follow her round the world. Of course, she couldn't give up her career.' Caroline turned away. 'It makes me sick, the way he gets away with it!'

'Away with what?' Jon asked.

Caroline turned to look at her. 'You should know. You're crazy about him, aren't you?' Her smile was malicious and Jon shuddered. 'Not that I should blame you,' Caroline added bitterly. 'We're all in the same boat.'

'You . . .' Jon began, startled.

Caroline laughed. 'I don't, but I did. Ten years ago before I met Samuel, I fell hook, line and sinker for Alex. I could have married him, but thank God I didn't.'

'Why thank God?' Jon asked.

Caroline's smile was bitter. 'Because I'd have had to take third place in his life. Alex has two loves: himself and his sanctuary. Nothing matters but his work. I prefer to become first in my husband's life. Alex is everything I hate and yet I love . . . loved him. He's a perfectionist, but what right has he to talk? He wasn't all that good when he was young. He sowed his wild oats all right. Besides, he's a hypocrite. He's always talking about preserving wild life and that sort of hogwash, while the truth is he used to murder

199

animals for money.'

'Murder animals for money?' Jon repeated. Was Caroline drunk? she began to wonder.

'And how! He's all for the R.S.P.C.A., but at one time he was a white game hunter. He'd take wealthy Americans out and encourage them to shoot helpless animals who've never hurt anyone. He must have made a pile of money out of killing them, and if that isn't bestial cruelty, what is? He's ruthless and cruel. The absolute egoist!' Caroline paused for breath and perhaps saw the shocked look on Jon's face, for she laughed, 'Sorry, Jon, for blowing my top, but he makes me so mad. Now I'd better go and do the hostess act. My darling husband who puts me first in his life does like me to do my duty.'

Jon was hardly alone for a moment when Tim joined her.

'Well, have you seen Alex's latest bird?' Tim asked as he swept Jon on to the floor as the music started. 'Quite an eyeful. It looks as if he finds her a pleasant armful, too,' he added as they danced by Alex, who was dancing with Antonia Herd, he smiling down at her and she gazing adoringly at him.

That inscrutable smile of Alex's, Jon thought, that told you nothing. You never knew if it was a smile of amusement, contempt, sarcasm, or affection. The most hateful smile, that promised everything, and gave you nothing.

'I'm . . . It's terribly hot in here. Could we sit in the garden?'

He smiled and danced her off the floor. 'Nothing I'd like more, darling.'

It was just bad luck that they stood still by Alex's side. He smiled at them.

'Jon, I want you to meet . . .' he turned to the beautiful girl by his side, 'Antonia, I'd like you to meet Jon Hampton. You've heard me talk of Uncle Ned?'

The lovely girl pulled a wry face. 'And how! I used to get bored to tears, dearest, because you never stopped talking about Uncle Ned. Are you a relation of his?' she asked Jon.

'His niece,' said Jon, fascinated by the friendliness of the smile on the girl's face.

'Of course,' Antonia nodded. 'You inherited the farm Alex wanted to buy.'

'Wants,' Tim butted in.

Antonia looked at him thoughtfully, but didn't speak. She turned to Jon. 'And you refuse to sell it to Alex? The courage!' she laughed. 'I suppose you're another victim of his charm?'

It was Alex who laughed. 'On the contrary, we're enemies.' He smiled at Jon—that slow smile she hated. 'Aren't we, little Jon?'

Jon smiled back. 'If you say so, Alex. Of course you're always right.' She turned to Tim. 'Come on, Tim darling, let's go where we can breathe,' she said, and walked off the patio, towards the dark trees. She was trembling with

201

anger. How dared Alex treat her like that in front of people?

*   *   *

As the evening passed, Jon danced mostly with Tim. She saw that Alex danced with Antonia most of the time, too. She caught a glimpse of Madeleine's pale sulky face as she tossed back her golden hair and laughed at her partner, a sturdily-built eighteen-year-old who was painfully shy. Madeleine was looking beautiful in a long frock that matched her hair, but her eyes were miserably sad as she watched Alex dance by, Antonia in his arms.

Jon caught her breath. If she was jealous of Antonia—and Madeleine was, too, then what about her own mother? she wondered. She looked round anxiously. Bless her, she thought, for her mother was putting on as brave a face as Jon herself was trying to do! Her mother was dancing with that old Colonel who was teaching her bridge and whom she was obviously sorry for. He was a widower and lonely, her mother had once said.

The sympathy and understanding in Jon made her see her mother as a woman, perhaps for the first time—a woman whose heart could be broken, whose hopes raised and then dropped, who could be loved and later forgotten. A woman like herself. Suddenly Jon wanted to go to her mother, to comfort her, to

202

promise her that she would get over it, that you always do—just as Kirsty had tried to comfort her.

It was nearly midnight and they formed a circle, crossing hands, and she found her hand clasped firmly by Alex. Startled, she looked up at him, but he was not smiling. He gave her a long thoughtful look, almost a concerned look, she thought for a moment, then told herself she must be imagining it. Alex was certainly not concerned about her! As they danced in a circle, laughing and singing *Auld Lang Syne*, Jon was only conscious of the firm but impersonal touch of Alex's fingers.

As the singing stopped, he looked down at her. 'What's happened to your voice, little Jon? I didn't hear you singing.'

Her cheeks burned as he could always make them do. 'Didn't I?' she asked, then smiled sweetly. 'Perhaps you're growing deaf.'

Antonia, on his other side, burst out laughing.

'How lovely! Alex, you are growing white, you know.' She caressed the side of his head. 'I love white-haired men,' she added.

Alex laughed. 'Watch your step. I know your age, remember?'

She laughed up at him. 'I can trust you not to betray my secret, dearest. Shouldn't we be drinking champagne to toast the New Year?'

In the consequent movement round the room, Jon tried to slip away, but Tim found her and made her stand in a group with the Oswalds, laughing and joking. Inside her, Jon wondered what would happen in the new year that lay ahead. Would she still be here next December the thirty-first? Would she be living with her mother? Would she have a stepfather who was the man she loved so much? Would she have given in and sold him the farm?

No, a thousand times no. She owed so much to Uncle Ned that she could never let him down. He had said never sell the farm to Alex. And that was one thing Jon knew that she would never do. She might be forced to sell the farm one day—but it never would be to Alex!

CHAPTER TEN

The days passed and the holidays were over; the children, most of them at boarding school, vanished and life returned to normal. Tim and Jon visited the Oswalds a lot; Jon painted, gardened, and her love for the blue mountains became almost an obsession. She grew accustomed to waking soon after four each morning and lying in bed, watching through the window the magic of sunrise—the palest green streaks, the soft gold, the pink shades. Sometimes she slept again, but more often she got up, put on jeans and a thin old shirt and sandals and slipped out of the house, the dogs with her. This was the best part of the day, she found. How could she bear to leave now she had grown to love it all so much? Jabula meant happiness. If only it could have meant that for her!

Everything seemed to be going smoothly. Occasionally Tim came to her with the suggestion of buying a new truck or some other thing they needed. He would always discuss it seriously, pointing out that money spent like that was an investment, for the more pineapples they could handle and sell, the more money they would make.

One day Jon had driven her mother to Qwaleni to meet some friends and had then gone shopping, still searching for a book on first aid. Alex had, it seemed, forgotten his promise to lend her one. Her study of Violet and Dorcas's language was not very successful. She practised with them, asking them to show her how to pronounce the difficult words, but she saw how hard it was for them not to laugh at her!

'Jon!' a cold voice said curtly.

Alex! she thought with a strange mixture of joy and dismay. She was growing used to Alex's infuriating habit of sneaking up behind her and had controlled her start.

'Good morning,' she said with equal coldness as she turned to face him.

They stared at one another silently for a moment, then Alex spoke.

'I want to talk to you alone, Jon. Can you meet me in half an hour at the Karrafin Café? It's urgent.'

'Urgent?' she echoed, and nodded. 'I'll be there.'

'Thanks.' He turned away abruptly and left her.

Jon glanced at her watch and wandered round the shop, idly turning pages but not seeing a word she read, for her thoughts were jumbled. Alex had sounded serious. What could have happened?

It was with her usual wariness that she went to the café and found Alex already there, although she was ten minutes early. He had chosen a table under a large sun-umbrella and asked her if she would prefer a cold drink or coffee.

She dabbed at her face with a tissue. As fast as she put on make-up, the perspiration streamed down her face and spoilt her looks. 'Cold drink, please.'

Alex smiled. 'It is hot,' he said sympathetically. 'Hotter than where we live. Mind, I'm higher than you, so I do get the wind—when there is any.'

They talked of unimportant things until the cold drinks arrived and they were alone and then Alex's face changed and became grave.

'Jon, are you doing anything about preparing the guest house for Dean?'

Surprised and puzzled, Jon shook her head.

206

'I haven't thought of it. He seems quite happy living with us.'

Alex's mouth was a thin line as if he was controlling anger.

'I'm sure he is, but that's another matter. Surely it's struck you that your mother won't always want to live in Jabula? She never has liked it. I think, too, that she's met so many friends of Uncle Ned that she begins to realize she misjudged him and this makes her feel guilty and unhappy in his home. Guilt is an unpleasant companion.'

'She was very young when Dad died,' Jon said quickly, leaping to her mother's defence. 'And she loved him very much.'

'I'm aware of that,' Alex said coldly. 'The point is—has it struck you that she might be thinking of marrying again?'

There was a silence so tense that Jon could scarcely breathe. A silence that grew and grew, but she could not say a word. So this was the moment—the moment when Alex was going to tell her he loved her mother and they were to be married.

She clutched the arms of her chair and stared at him. His face was a blur.

'I . . . I . . . I had wondered . . .' she managed to say. 'I hope . . .'

Alex frowned impatiently. 'She's in no hurry, of course. Her main trouble is you. She can't just walk out and leave you alone in the house with Tim Dean. The local gossip is bad enough now without you adding to it.'

'When will the wedding be?' Jon asked, her voice almost a whisper.

Alex shrugged. 'Nothing's been decided yet. There's no hurry, but you're holding her back and I'm sure that's the last thing you want to do. After all, you've been wanting your independence for a long time, haven't you?' he added with a cold smile.

'I want her to be happy,' Jon said quickly.

Alex smiled. 'Well, that's settled that. I take it you'll have the guest house tackled immediately?'

She nodded. Inside her, words churned angrily together. She wanted to accuse him of trying to cheat her—ask him if it was true about the dam going to be built and the high compensation payment she would get? She wanted to tell him that she could no longer trust him. That Uncle Ned had warned her ...

Half closing her eyes, she corrected herself. Uncle Ned had not warned her *against* Alex. He had said Alex could be trusted. How wrong he was!

A quiet ominous rumble broke the stillness and Jon looked up at the sky. A few dark clouds were collecting on the horizon. She wanted to get home before the storm broke ...

She picked up her handbag, but Alex put out his hand and took it away.

'I haven't finished yet,' he said coldly.

She looked round her, wishing she could

escape. The slight breeze that had welcomed them had suddenly vanished and the heat seemed to press down on her. The bright sunshine made her eyes and head ache—or was it Alex? she wondered.

He leant forward. 'Jon, I feel it my duty to tell you that the costs of running your farm have risen considerably since Dean started to work for you. He is buying unnecessary vehicles, wasting your money.'

Jon looked at him. 'I am aware of his purchases,' she said stiffly. 'Tim orders nothing without my consent. We always discuss it first. We are investing money in . . . in things we'll need in the future.'

'What future?'

Jon bit her lower lip, trying not to lose her temper. 'The future of Jabula—or are you still hoping I'll sell it to you?' She leaned forward over the table, her control vanishing. 'I never will, Alex Roe, that I swear. No matter what you do to me, steal my boys, sabotage everything, I'll never sell to *you* . . .'

For a moment, he looked shocked. 'I haven't asked you to sell to me,' he said, his voice icy. 'I am no longer interested in it.'

'That's a lie. If you don't want to ruin me, why are you stealing all our best workers?'

Alex's eyes narrowed, but a smile played round his mouth. 'So that's what you think? Or did Dean suggest it to you? I'm stealing your best workers?' He laughed. 'My dear little Jon, just how gullible can you be? I have workers I've had for years. I don't want yours. If they prefer to work for me rather than for Dean, is it my fault?'

Jon could hardly speak. 'It is your fault. Why didn't you tell me about the dam?'

'The dam?'

'You know very well what I mean.' Jon found herself thumping the table with her fist. 'If the dam is built, they'll pay me compensation, but you want that compensation, don't you? That's why you're trying to make me sell the farm to you. All you think of is money. Haven't you got enough? Why must you . . . why must you . . .' She pressed her hand against her mouth, for the tears were painfully near and her voice unsteady.

'So that's what you believe of me,' Alex said slowly. There was no anger in his voice. No pain. No contradiction. Just acceptance. 'I can see you've been well brainwashed. Jon, I didn't tell you before as Dean had just started with you and I knew how much it meant to you to get rid of me, but that little cat of yours, I found it on the Repan Rock.'

Jon stared at him, shocked. 'But how did she get there?'

'Exactly. She must have been put there. You may remember that Dean said he hadn't known the cat was yours—that he thought it was a stray. Doesn't that add up? Or are you so crazily in love with him that you're wilfully blind?'

'You mean—you think Tim put her there—to starve to death?'

Repan Rock was a local landmark—a huge rock, shaped vaguely like a lion's head, surrounded by a wide stream of deep water that ran fast before starting on its journey down the mountain side. 'No, he would never do such a thing.'

'The heat would have killed the cat. That's the sort of man your precious Tim is.' Alex's voice lost its cold impersonal note as he showed his anger.

'I don't believe it!' Jon stared at him defiantly. 'You're making it all up. Tim isn't a murderer . . . like you were,' she added, startled as she heard what she had said and wondering if she had gone too far.

But Alex merely looked puzzled and then his face broke into a smile. 'I see. Caroline has been talking to you. Why? I thought she'd given me up years ago. She's never forgiven me, you know. She wanted us to marry and go to England. I had to tell her that I didn't love her. In those days I was as naïve as you are today.'

'That's not what she told me.'

Alex laughed. 'I bet it isn't! Did she say she refused to marry me because my work came first? The second part was true, but not the first. I never loved her.'

How cruelly, how coldly he said it, Jon thought. He just doesn't care how many hearts he breaks.

'She said you killed animals for money— that you took wealthy Americans on safari trips and murdered harmless creatures. Was it monkeys?'

Alex shook his head. 'I was very young when I shot my first monkey. Never again. They cry like a baby—terrible. Lions, elephants are more my mark.'

There was another ominous rumble of thunder and Alex stood up. 'You'd better get going before the storm does.' He called the waiter and paid for the cold drinks and walked with Jon to her car.

'I'll be coming along in an hour's time so if you get into trouble, just wait for me.'

He said it impersonally, almost as if talking to a complete stranger, she thought as she drove away.

She drove quickly but carefully, thinking of what Alex had said, and anger grew again inside her. How he hated poor Tim! He was always trying to make Tim seem bad when all the time it was Alex . . .

Or was it? She found it hard to believe that Alex could be so mean, so cruel and hard. Yet she knew it from experience, didn't she? she asked herself. A man of many moods. A man you could never understand—only love. And where did that get you?

Why hadn't he told her the whole story when he talked of her mother remarrying? Why . . .

She slowed down as a herd of goats ran down the rocky hillside and strolled over the road. A small baby goat stood still in the middle and stared at her. Then down came a little African boy, waving his minute stick.

Why did she keep asking *herself* all these questions but never the people concerned? she asked herself. Perhaps her mother would welcome a question, perhaps it would give her an opening . . .

That evening her mother was staying in and Jon invented a headache, so Tim went out alone. He never stayed at the house in the evening if he could avoid it, she realized.

It seemed strange to be alone with her mother again, almost like the old days in Bexhill. After dinner, they sat on the stoep, small coils burning to keep away the mosquitoes. Her mother was knitting a pullover, an attractive shade of grey. Jon tucked her feet under her, linking her thin fingers together.

'Mum,' she said abruptly, 'why didn't you tell me you were thinking of getting married?'

Her mother looked up, dropped a stitch but ignored it.

'How did you know, Jon?'

'Alex told me.'

'Alex?' Her mother frowned. 'But why . . . ?'

'He said I must get the guest house ready for Tim, because after you go, I can't be alone in the house with him.'

'Alex said that?' Her mother carefully picked up the dropped stitch, folded up the knitting, clasped her hands and looked at her daughter. 'Jon, would you mind very much if I did marry? I'm not so young and I often get lonely. One day you'll get married and I'll have no one. He's such a darling and he needs someone to look after him. I'm sure you can see that?'

'I suppose so . . .' Jon said slowly, trying to imagine Alex needing to be looked after! Maybe love made her mother wish that to be true and had made herself believe it.

'When are you getting married? Alex said you were in no hurry. He blames me for . . . for that. He says you feel you can't leave me alone with . . .'

Her mother smiled. 'Darling, Alex is so right. I might have married long ago, only I wanted to see you happily married first. I'm glad, though, I waited. I'm sure we're going to be very happy. The only thing is, darling, I'll miss you terribly.'

Jon stared at her, puzzled, and then understood. Alex was sure that once he had married her mother, Jon would let them have the farm and go away. That was what he planned. Perhaps that was why he was marrying her mother? Caroline had said he was ruthless and cruel.

'I'm going away soon to meet his family, Jon, and . . .'

'I thought his parents were dead.'

'Oh, they are. What he calls his family are the three children he had by his first marriage. His wife died, you see, and they live with his brother.'

'I didn't know he'd been married before?'

What a dark horse Alex was! Hiding everything as if there was something to be ashamed of. But Alex with three children . . .

'Will they live with you? The children, I mean?'

Her mother smiled. 'I doubt it. They're in their late teens. Anyhow, we'll see.' She stood up. 'I'm so glad we've had this little talk, darling, and you've taken it so well. I was a bit afraid you'd be hurt.'

Jon hugged her mother. 'Of course not, darling,' she lied. 'Why should I be hurt? I'm only glad you're so happy.'

'I wasn't sure at first. I thought the difference in our ages was too great, but the more I know him, the more I . . . well, maybe this sounds odd coming from an oldie as I must seem to you, but I love him dearly and I think—in fact, I'm sure—we'll be very happy.'

'Oh, Mum, I'm so glad . . . for you,' Jon said, and kissed her, turning away quickly, afraid lest her mother see the tears in her eyes. 'Is it a secret or is the engagement going to be announced?'

'A secret, of course. Please don't tell anyone at all, Jon. We plan a quiet wedding and if everyone knew . . . well, we'd have to ask everyone. So not a word.'

'Not a word,' Jon promised.

Alone in her bedroom, she gazed in the mirror. Had she lost weight? Her face looked thinner. Her mouth turned down at the corners. She looked exactly what she was—an idiot drowned in self-pity. She should be ashamed. Think of all the unhappy years her mother had known, the shock of losing a beloved husband so soon, the loneliness, the fact that she was growing older every day— surely she was entitled to happiness? After all, Jon told herself, she was young. Only twenty-three. There would be years ahead of her.

If only . . . She flung herself on the bed, hugging the pillow tightly, keeping her eyes shut. How could she bear it? Would she be a bridesmaid? Kissed by the bridegroom after the ceremony? Laughing, wishing them happiness, watching them go, alone together and for always? How could she do it?

CHAPTER ELEVEN

One week later, Tim asked Jon to be his wife. Despite the gossip, Kirsty's advice and Alex's accusations, all the same it came as a surprise—perhaps because it had been such a strange day for Jon, a confused day, mixed with fear and reassurance, with love and hate.

The day began with heavy rain, grey skies and the mountains hidden behind heavy mists. There was a surprising coldness in the air, a chill that seemed to penetrate the pale blue cardigan Jon wore over a thin white shirt. She was wearing denim jeans too because they might be warmer. The weather changed so fast —the day before had been so swelteringly hot, yet today . . . She shivered.

The dogs were restless, so she played a game with them, throwing a small ball up and down the stoep. The floor was highly polished, so the dogs skidded as they tried to stop or leap after the ball. They loved the game and it was better than taking them out in the thick mud.

Her mother was to be fetched by a neighbour for lunch and a bridge session.

'I always seem to be out these days, darling,' Ursula said, a little wistfully. Although they had not talked of her approaching wedding since that night of honesty, somehow they were much closer and Jon felt again that her mother loved her.

'By the way, Jon, why are you having the guest house painted?'

Jon grabbed hold of the rubber ball, ignoring the dogs' eager thrusts as they waited impatiently for the game to continue.

'Why, Mum, didn't I tell you that Alex told me to?'

"Alex? Was it his idea?"

'Yes. He said that after you had gone, Tim would have to sleep there.'

'Of course. I'd forgotten. Jon . . .' her mother hesitated for a moment, 'Are you in love with Tim?'

Jon shrugged her shoulders. 'I'm fond of him, but love . . .' Suddenly she wondered if it might make it easier for her mother if she believed that Jon was in love with Tim and that one day they might be married. 'I'm not sure, Mum. I haven't known him long, and besides,' she smiled, 'he hasn't asked me.'

A long grey car came into the drive. 'He will,' said Ursula. 'But be very sure before you say yes, darling. Tim is a dear boy, but . . .'

'I promise I won't rush into it, Mum. We'll be engaged for at least six months.'

'Good, darling. Somehow I thought . . .'

The woman behind the driving wheel of the car gave an impatient hoot and Ursula laughed.

'Coming!' she called, and Jon held an umbrella over her as they ran to the car.

Jon waved goodbye and walked back into the house slowly.

The dogs came racing to meet her. Even old Jocky, who had taken so long to accept her, came now, wagging his tail. Throwing the ball, squeezing it out of the dogs' mouths if they refused to drop it, passed the time, Jon thought. Later she would study her language book and ask Dorcas if she was pronouncing the words correctly. Suddenly she wondered where Tim was. Probably out on the lands somewhere, though as a rule he stayed indoors when it rained hard, leaving it to the *induna* to cope.

At that moment Dorcas jerked open the house door and stood, breathless and frightened.

'Jonah's cut his hand, missis. Very bad cut with much blood.'

'I'll come,' said Jon, leaving the dogs on the stoep as they would only jump about, barking and perhaps alarming Jonah, one of the farm hands.

She took the first aid box and hurried through the kitchen. Jonah, a short thin man, was squatting on the small porch, sheltered from the worst of the rain, holding the damaged hand by the wrist and watching the blood dripping to the ground . . .

At the same moment, a truck came round behind the house and drew up. Jon saw with mixed dismay and relief that it was Alex. He came striding through the rain, ankle deep in the mud. Would he stand and watch her cope, she wondered—or take over?

She might have known which he'd do! 'I'll cope with this,' he said gruffly. 'Go and put on a mackintosh, Jon, and boots. Where on earth is this manager of yours?'

'Out on the lands,' said Jon, standing back and watching Alex quickly wash his hands before coping with Jonah.

'More likely asleep in his bed,' Alex said sourly. 'Get going, Jon. We've no time to waste. Get your mackintosh, I've something to show you.'

Jon hesitated. 'Mum's out.'

'I know that. Hurry, we've no time to spare.'

'Why.'

Alex straightened. 'Look, Jon, do I have to spell it out? Be quick about it!' he snapped.

Jon turned and obeyed, thrusting her bare feet into the small wellington boots, pulling on her mackintosh and tying a scarf round her head and hurrying back to the kitchen, wondering what it was Alex wanted to show her. Was it something to do with Tim?

Alex was waiting impatiently, telling the girls something.

'I ought to leave a note . . .' Jon began.

'There isn't time. I've told them.' Alex's hand gripped her arm and he almost thrust her in front of him through the heavy rain and mud to the truck. Now she could see that two of Alex's workers were squatting in the back under a tarpaulin, and that each had a rifle.

He almost pushed her into the truck, then ran round and climbed up into the driver's seat, switched on the ignition and drove over

220

the squelching mud round the house and out through the gate.

'Where are we going?' Jon asked.

'Wait and see.'

Alex didn't speak again for the first hour. Nor did Jon. She could see how angry he was, but with whom she didn't know. Was it with her? With Tim? Who? She sat, hunched up, for it was cold as the truck swerved and jerked on the bad earth road, skidding, sliding perilously near the long drops as they climbed the mountains and slid down into the valleys again. The rain pelted down so that the windscreen wipers found it hard to work, and then, without warning, the rain stopped and she saw that they were driving into a dry area. It was even more strange when they began to send up clouds of dust behind them.

'They've had no rain here,' she said wonderingly.

Alex didn't turn his head. 'Obviously,' he said.

After that she stayed quiet for a long time. It was getting hotter and hotter as they went lower down in the huge valley. She struggled out of her mackintosh and pushed the scarf into one of the pockets. Then she wiped the dust off her face with an old tissue.

'Is it much farther?' she asked as the silence became unbearable.

'Not much.'

Suddenly she could stand it no longer.

'What's wrong, Alex? Why are you so mad about something?'

'I'm not mad. I'm furious.'

'Well, furious, then. Where are we going and why?'

He slowed up and she saw a high wire fence with an entrance and someone who came out of a small but to unlock the gates.

'Is this a game reserve?'

'Precisely,' he said curtly.

They drove more slowly along the wide track, past trees and bushes, but she saw no animals.

As if he could read her thoughts, he said: 'Too hot for them to be about. The early morning is the best time.'

'Then why have we come now?'

He turned to look at her and she had never seen such anger on his face before. 'We have come,' he said very slowly, 'to shoot a lion.'

'What? You're going to . . . to shoot a lion?' Jon almost gasped.

He smiled, a smile without amusement. 'You called me a murderer for money—or perhaps those were Caroline's words. I thought you might like to see what happens, only this time I don't get paid for it.'

'But . . .' she began, then stopped, for they had gone into another wire surrounded area only this time, there was a small, single-storied house that was half hidden by purple bougainvillea flowers. Even as they stopped, the front door opened and a girl came out. She looked about twenty with red hair and a weary frightened face.

'Alex!' she said, almost tumbling down the steps to meet him. 'I don't know how to thank you. I've had to fight Mike to keep him in bed and his temperature is a hundred and five. Could you see him and make him realize . . .' Suddenly she must have seen Jon, for she looked startled. 'Would you like a cup of coffee?'

Jon nodded and slid down from the high truck. Alex had already vanished into the house and the two girls followed.

'I've just made us some coffee, so it's lucky,' the girl said, then laughed. 'Oh, dear, I don't know if I'm on my head or my heels! My name is Nancy Kirkwood and my husband is a game warden, but he's ill with 'flu and he's a bit bronchitis-inclined, so I've got to look after him. Last year he had pneumonia . . . and there's an absolute epidemic here of 'flu and . . .' She rubbed a hand wearily over her face. 'So I phoned Alex. He never lets us down.'

Jon, sipping the hot sweet coffee, began to speak. 'But why . . .' but she had no chance to finish the sentence, for Alex returned and took the cup out of her hand.

'We must get going. Mike sees sense, Nancy. I'm taking his guide to show me where the lion is.'

'Shouldn't she . . . I don't know your name

. . . shouldn't she stay with me, Alex?' Nancy asked worriedly. 'Mike will never take me along.'

'This is different. Jon wants to see a kill,' Alex said his voice grim.

'No, I . . .' Jon began, but again was given no chance as Alex pulled her along, forcing her outside and almost throwing her up into the truck as a short African jumped up in the back and spoke to the other two men and then the truck jerked forward.

Jon felt sick as she sat still. How could Alex be so cruel? She had no desire to see a poor lion slaughtered. Why must they kill him? Why couldn't the lion go on living? Wasn't that what game reserves were for? she thought, but, glancing at Alex, she decided this was not the right moment to talk to him.

They drove some distance along the main road but saw nothing, and then as the guide leaned over from the back and shouted at Alex, the truck left the road and jolted its way across what was little more than a track. Jon looked round her miserably, dreading what lay ahead. Even the sight of a group of monkeys squatting on the ground, staring at them, didn't ease her misery.

Finally Alex swung the steering wheel round and stopped under a group of trees. He jumped down and came round to her side. His face was grim, his mouth a thin line. He had a rifle in his hand.

'Stay put,' he ordered curtly. 'Lions are not socially minded. Keep the window shut.'

She watched him as he, the guide and one other man walked slowly through the thick yellow grass. Looking back, she saw that the other man was standing up in the truck, his rifle ready. Was he there to protect her? she wondered.

She shivered. Alex had said that lions were not socially minded. Neither were elephants. Suppose one walked out on to . . .

She caught her breath as fear went through her. Was Alex mad? Anything could happen to him. Suppose the lion was hiding and then leapt . . .

She was so frightened for him that she began to wind down the window to shout at him, to get him to let the poor lion live, not to risk his life. Then she realized that she was getting hysterical, so she closed the window and buried her face in her hands, for she couldn't bear to watch Alex walking to . . . to, perhaps, his death.

The sudden roar of an angry lion jerked up her head and opened her eyes. She could no longer see the three men, they had vanished, but suddenly Alex appeared from behind a bush, glancing back at the truck, lifted his hand to give the V-sign of victory, and strangely, her fear for him went. Suddenly she knew that he knew what he was doing . . . now it was the lion she felt sorry for.

Another angry roar made her jump, made her glad the windows were closed, that someone in the truck was watching.

There was a third roar. A strange sound, almost, she thought, a desperate sound. She leaned against the glass, gazing anxiously now towards the bushes where Alex was hiding.

Suddenly she saw the lion—a great beast walking strangely as if limping. His tail was swinging, his head rolling from side to side, then as he came out of the long grass and she could see him plainly she saw why he was hobbling. His fourth leg was being dragged helplessly as he made his way on three legs. He must have been hurt, she realized, and at that moment Alex stepped forward and she heard a shot . . .

The lion gave a stifled roar, moved forward, falling over in the same moment, jerked his legs and then lay very still. Jon sat very still, fighting the sickness that filled her as she watched Alex move cautiously to the dead animal's side, bend down, then stand up and walk towards her.

He jerked open the truck door. 'I want to show you something,' he said curtly.

'I don't want to . . . to see it . .' she began, but Alex was not listening. He literally pulled her down and half carried her across the patch of dry earth to where the lion lay.

'No, Alex, I won't look!' she said, struggling.

'You will—if we have to stand here ten

hours,' he said angrily.

She knew he meant what he said and that in this mood all the arguments or tears would have no effect. But as she gazed at the dead lion, she cried out, clapping her hand to her mouth with horror. The damaged leg was terribly torn with deep cuts, covered with dried blood and ants and flies. The lion's mouth was badly torn, too, his jaw hanging down loosely.

'How did it happen?' she gasped, turning her head away, trying not to be sick.

'A poacher's trap,' Alex said, and he half carried her back to the truck, lifting her up and going round to sit by her side. 'Wire, Jon. He must have torn himself to bits trying to get free. He broke his jaw and couldn't run, so could find no animal he could kill. Desperate with pain and hunger, he must have forced his way into a kraal and found a small child playing in the dust.'

Alex paused, looking at Jon's white face. Then he pulled a flask from the pocket at the side of the truck and a glass and filled it, giving it to her.

'Drink it slowly,' he ordered, and went on as she obeyed: 'You can guess what followed. He ate the child. It wasn't his fault . . . it's that . . .' Alex clamped his mouth as if afraid to let himself say what he wanted to. 'Feel better?' he asked abruptly.

Jon nodded. The drink burned her throat but was warming her.

'Sorry . . . silly of me.'

'Nonsense.' For a moment he smiled. 'I thought you were going to black out. I didn't realize it would be such a shock.'

She shivered. 'He must have been in agony.'

'I'm sure he was. That's why I came out. A wounded beast has to be shot quickly—not only to spare him further agony but to protect the children.' He sighed. 'When I think . . . It's the game warden's job, but when they're sick, I lend a hand.'

Jon glanced across the bare patch and saw that the three Africans were slowly dragging the lion along the ground.

'What will they do with him?'

Alex smiled grimly. 'Eat him, of course. We'll get going as soon as they get him on the truck.'

It was a slow business, for the animal was a heavy one. Jon tried not to look at that blood-covered face, not to think of his panic as he was trapped, the agony he suffered.

At last they were able to get away and Alex drove back to the main road, stopping at a small clearing where there were a few thatched huts with a fence round them. Four or five women came running, with small children clinging to their skirts.

'They don't usually have lions down here, but there's been a long drought,' Alex explained as the lion was pulled off, hitting the ground with a heavy thump. 'And they've come in search of water. That's how he got caught in a cunningly-laid trap.'

Gradually as Alex talked more and more, some of the nausea left Jon and she could relax and listen to what he said as he drove the truck. She had to sit close to him as otherwise he had to shout above the noise of the engine. She was fascinated by what he told her.

'Life as a game warden is exciting and interesting, but there are tough moments. If too many elephants are bred, they destroy the trees and, in this way, make life impossible for other animals, so we have to make a regular check on the number of elephants or else the reserve will become a dust-heap. It's the same with lions. We have to know how many there are because, of course, they live off the other animals and if the number gets out of hand ...' He shrugged.

'And if there are too many?' she asked.

'We shoot them.' He glanced at her. 'It's a quick death, Jon, and better than letting them die starving or caught in a trap.'

Later he talked about his sanctuary and his plans.

'That reminds me, Caroline said I organized safaris? I thought so. The truth is I only went on one in my life. Certainly it was with Americans, wealthy all of them. I did go to shoot—but my weapon was a camera.' He chuckled as he looked at her face. 'Some time—if you won't be too bored—you must

229

see my films.'

Alex talked to her as he had never talked before. Relaxed, he told her about the animals that were rescued when the Kariba Dam was built; he explained about the arrows that were shot into wild animals and that sent them to sleep long enough so that they might be examined to see if they were healthy, or to move them to a less crowded part of the reserve.

She felt quite sorry when she recognized the road to the valley where she lived. Alex must have noticed it, too, for his whole behaviour changed. He became serious.

'I'm sorry I was difficult on the outward trip, Jon, but I was so angry I could barely trust myself to speak. I felt I might explode and use language that would startle you.' He smiled. 'I'd hate to shock you!' Then his smile vanished and she saw his hands clenched round the steering wheel. 'You know, Jon, when I think of what those poachers do, I feel I'd like to kill them with my own hands.' His voice was unsteady for a moment. 'Kill if they must, but not by slow torture.'

Jon turned to him impulsively. She had not long, because they were under the jacarandas and would soon be home.

'I owe you an apology, too, Alex. I shouldn't have believed what Caroline said. I should have known better and trusted you.'

He smiled. 'Well, while we're apologizing, I

should say I'm sorry I forced you to watch the kill.'

'But it wasn't a kill, Alex. It was an act of mercy, to put him out of pain. I didn't realize there were poachers and such things happened. I didn't realize the awfulness of it all.'

He drove round the back of the house and helped her down from the truck. 'How could you know? This is a totally different world.'

She watched the truck until it was gone from sight, then went slowly indoors, conscious of her tiredness, and the need for a bath or shower.

Tim came striding into the empty kitchen, his face furious.

'Where the devil have you been? I was worried sick.'

'Tim, I'm sorry. We told the girls.'

'You could have left me a note.'

'Tim, there wasn't time. We had to find the lion and shoot it.'

'Lion? What on earth are you talking about?'

She followed him into the lounge, describing the awfulness. 'That poor lion— what he must have suffered!' she finished.

'Sounds daft to me, Jon. The lion would have died in the end.'

She stared at him. 'But he was starving and in agony. He'd killed a baby . . .'

'And gave wonderful Alex Roe the chance to

231

look like a hero. Why didn't one of the game wardens shoot it?'

'They're all ill.'

He caught hold of her shoulders and looked at her. 'Jon, will you marry me?' he said bluntly.

She was close to him. She could see the two freckles on his longish nose, the way his mouth curled down, the longish hair. But she saw a stranger, no longer the pleasant amusing helpful Tim she had grown fond of—the man holding her shoulders was just a stranger. A man who could put a little cat where it could only die in agony—a man who said let the lion die, again in agony. What sort of man was this? How could she have believed all he said? Letting him make her doubt a man like Alex, persuading her to believe lies.

'I'm sorry, Tim, but . . .' She tried to free herself, but his hands gripped her.

'I thought you loved me,' he said accusingly. 'We've been everywhere together.'

'That doesn't always mean marriage. Please, Tim, you're hurting me!' He let her go and she rubbed her shoulders. 'Look, Tim, I like you a lot, an awful lot, but marriage . . .'

'You're in love with Alex Roe, aren't you?'

She felt her cheeks burning. 'I am not! In any case . . .' she began, then stopped suddenly, remembering that her mother had asked her not to tell anyone.

'What has he got that I haven't?' Tim

demanded. 'Money? Is that what you girls are after? Or do you like his arrogance, his sarcasm, his showmanship? There must be something that attracts you all!'

He turned away and went to his room, slamming the door angrily. Jon stared after him. She hated having to hurt him, but he mustn't have even the smallest hope, for she knew that there could only be one man for her—Alex Roe. And if she could not have him, then she would remain a spinster for life!

Soaking in the bath, she went over Alex's words on the truck. How easily he had talked to her, not once had he teased her. If only he was always like that!

She closed her eyes, remembering something he had said that she would never forget and that helped her understand his absorption in his sanctuary.

'A true hunter must be a naturalist, Jon. He must love the wild, his animals, his bushveld, his mountains, his birds and the wild flowers and trees. He must love it all. A true hunter needs a strong heart, a sharp eye, natural reactions and quick reflexes. It's a great life, Jon, although it can be tough.'

She went over the words again and again, for that was how she felt. She loved the beautiful mountains, the gay little coloured birds who flitted from flower to flower, who sang such odd tunes; she loved the dogs, the cattle, even the tiresome goats. She loved the trees, too.

Alex's words had been a revelation. They had shown her a different kind of man from what she had thought him. And it made her love him more. Maybe, she told herself, maybe in time she could learn to love him as a stepfather instead of as a man.

Her mother came back as she was dressing. Jon was glad, for she rather dreaded Tim's reactions. However, they had a quiet evening for a change, for the rain that had stopped at lunch time had begun again and the roads were pretty bad, so Tim decided to stay at home for once. He was his usual amusing self, but all the time Jon was conscious that he was looking at her. And not with love.

Was it hate or contempt? she wondered.

CHAPTER TWELVE

Next morning when Jon woke, the sun was streaming in her room. Rex was wandering around restlessly and Dorcas brought in a cup of coffee. Jon drank it quickly, had a hasty shower and then took the dogs for their usual walk.

How beautiful everything was—so pristine fresh with the sparkles of rain water still on the leaves and flowers. That was, if you ignored the ankle-deep mud on which she kept slipping and sliding!

As she walked, she thought of Alex and all the things he had talked about. Now she could understand his love for his sanctuary, his desire to fight the poachers, to protect the animals. She wondered for a moment if her mother would. When she got back to the house, she saw a strange car outside the door. Tim's was not there, but he often drove to distant parts of the lands and hated going in the truck which made his back ache, he said. But who could the stranger be? It was a beautiful white car, a Mercedes, too.

She slipped in the back way and hastily showered and pulled on her pink cotton frock, gazed in the mirror and pulled a face at her reflection. If only she could look her age, she thought ruefully. If only she could look twenty-three!

'Darling, are you there?' her mother called, a note of excitement in her voice.

'Coming, Mum!' Jon called. Would the visitor have breakfast with them, she wondered, and where was Tim? Usually they waited for him if he was late, but if there was a visitor . . .

She went out on to the stoep and stood still in amazement. She recognized the man. He was the old Colonel she had met before—the friend of her mother's who was teaching her bridge.

'Jon darling, I do want you to meet

Geoffrey.'

Jon smiled and held out her hand. 'The Colonel and I have met before.'

'I know, darling, but you didn't really meet him. I want you to get to know him well.'

Jon was staring, puzzled, at her mother, who sounded quite nervous.

'Shall we go in for breakfast, Jon? Geoffrey came early as we want to drive down to Big Bend today and must start early. Tim is late, but he can have his breakfast later.'

'Of course.'

They sat round the breakfast table in an awkward atmosphere of several speaking at once, laughing nervously, and then there being a long silence. Jon hunted in her brain for something to say to the old man that would interest him.

'Are you very good at bridge?' she asked.

Dorcas brought in the paw-paw and placed the plates before them.

'We don't have this in England,' the Colonel said. 'I think it's such a pity. Apparently they can't pack it or something.' He smiled at Jon. 'I'm not very good at bridge, but I enjoy it.'

'You're English?' she asked.

Her mother laughed. 'Very much so. He lives in one of those adorably converted oasthouses in Kent.'

Dorcas removed the plates and brought in a large plate of scrambled eggs and fried mushrooms.

'Your favourite, I know,' said Ursula, smiling at the Colonel.

He smiled back. 'You spoil me.'

'I enjoy it,' Jon's mother said with a sudden gay little laugh, then she leaned forward. 'Let's stop behaving like idiots. I've told Jon all about you, Geoffrey darling, and she quite understands.'

Jon saw a slow red flush come to his cheek and was startled by the nervous way he smiled at her. 'And you don't mind?' he asked earnestly.

Jon was puzzled. What was there for her to mind about? That he was teaching her mother to play bridge and taking her out for the day?

'Of course not,' she said politely.

The Colonel smiled. 'Bless you! I thought you might resent it if I took your lovely mother away.'

Jon was even more puzzled. After all, it was just for the day!

She looked at her mother, who smiled back. 'Geoffrey wants to take me to Big Bend to meet his children and as soon as the guest house is ready for Tim, darling, we'll be getting married. I hope you'll be our bridesmaid and Alex our best man.'

Jon stared at her. She couldn't speak for a moment. She looked at the Colonel and saw the nervousness in his smile and the wistful look in her mother's eyes.

It couldn't be true, she thought, feeling that

everything was rushing madly at her and she was too confused to think.

'I hope you'll be very happy,' she said, then thought how stiff it sounded. She jumped to her feet, went to her mother, put her arms round her and kissed her. 'I'm so happy for you, Mum. I know you've often been lonely and I always hoped one day you'd marry again.'

She saw her mother dab quickly at her eyes before she smiled.

'Bless you, darling, I knew you'd understand.'

Jon moved to the side of the aristocratic-looking, white-haired man, and kissed him gently on the cheek. 'Welcome to the family, Stepdaddy,' she said warmly.

'How very sweet of you!' He spoke huskily as if very emotional, and Jon thought they needed a gayer note.

'Pity it's breakfast time, Mum. We should celebrate this with champagne,' she said cheerfully.

'We'll do that at the wedding, darling. Just the four of us. Geoffrey and myself, you and Alex. It'll be lovely.' She glanced at her watch. 'I'd better go and get ready, Geoffrey.' She laughed and looked at Jon. 'He's a stickler for punctuality and is always ready half an hour before I am,' she said, and left the room.

They talked as they finished breakfast. Jon poured him a second cup of coffee and thought he was much nicer as she got to know him. There was a gentleness about him, also a wistfulness.

'The years since I retired have been lonely ones. My children hardly know me, because I had to leave them with my married brother as I didn't want to interrupt their schooling. Your mother is so lovely I can't believe my good luck.'

Suddenly Jon wanted to hug and kiss him and she knew he was going to be right for her mother.

'Excuse me a moment,' she said. 'Would you like to wait on the stoep?'

He smiled. 'You want a short chat with your mother? Understandable. Tell her she can be late for once.' He was chuckling as he went outside to the stoep.

Jon hurried to her mother's room. 'Mum darling, are you sure he's not too old for you?'

Her mother turned, her face more serene than Jon had ever seen.

'You're as old as your heart is, darling. In some ways he's younger than me. I need someone to fuss over and someone to fuss over me. We share the same interests. We'll travel round the world. He isn't all that old, you know. I'm forty-one and he's only ten years older. He's been very ill and had to retire from the Army early, also his hair went white when he was thirty. That's what makes him look older than he really is.'

Jon hesitated. 'Mum, I always thought . . .' It was difficult to put into words. She spread out her hands and pretended to look at her nails. 'Mum, I thought you were going to marry Alex.'

'*What?*' her mother cried out in amazement. 'You must be joking! Me marry Alex? Whatever made you think that?'

'Well, you've spent a lot of time together. I mean, he was always driving you to Qwaleni . . .'

'That was to see Geoffrey. He had a bad back and was under treatment and Alex used to drive me and fetch me back.'

'But I thought . . .'

Ursula patted her hair and straightened the charming ruby-red silk frock. 'I do hope his children like me,' she said worriedly, then turned to look at Jon. 'You were joking, darling, weren't you? I mean, about Alex. Whatever made you think he was in love with me? I'm years older than he is!'

'Only five years, Mum. It was . . . well, he always looked after you, and . . .'

Ursula laughed. 'Exactly. He treated me like a piece of delicate Dresden china. That told me that he saw me as an older woman. When a man loves a woman, he isn't that kind of attentive. Besides, we share no interests at all. I think he's crazy over his animals. With all his money he could have a wonderful life, but he prefers to bury himself here and . . .'

'But he's happy here.'

Her mother laughed. 'Fair enough! Let's hope the girl he marries will also be happy here, but it certainly isn't my cup of tea. Darling, I must go. See you much later tonight.'

Jon watched the long white car drive away and walked slowly back into the house, ignoring for once the dogs. She sat down heavily in a chair, staring ahead of her, just staring at nothing.

All these months she had been so sure that Alex loved her mother and that her mother loved Alex. How could she have been so stupid? Was it fear that had blinded her? Fear of not winning his love? Could fear invent a rival?

The telephone bell shrilled impatiently. Jon answered it. She sat very still, listening, and then asked him to repeat it again.

'Your farm manager has just cashed a cheque which leaves you very much in the red, Miss Hampton,' her bank manager said. 'Unfortunately I was engaged or I would have phoned you before allowing it to be paid. I thought you ought to know. You may have signed other cheques.'

'How much was it for?' Jon asked, puzzled. Why should Tim need to cash a cheque today? It wasn't pay day, nor had they ordered anything that required payment by cash. 'How much?' Her voice was horrified as she listened.

'I haven't signed a cheque for that amount!'

'Then it must be a forgery. I'll get on to the police,' he said crisply.

'But he wouldn't . . .' Jon felt stunned.

'I suggest you ring Mr Roe,' the bank manager said curtly. 'He's better at handling these things than you.'

'Yes, Mr Baker, I will—at once,' said Jon.

She stood up, her limbs suddenly heavy. It couldn't be true. Tim forging her signature? Cashing a cheque that size . . .

Somehow she walked to Tim's room and opened the door. In a few moments she knew he had gone. And so had the portable radio they had loaned him! All his clothes, his books, suitcases. Everything that was Tim's had gone, including, she suddenly noticed, the clock they had lent him with a strong alarm.

Tim . . . how could he do this to her? She walked back to the phone and rang Alex's number. The phone rang and rang, but there was no reply.

Jon went outside on the stoep and the dogs leapt to greet her, but she stood still, unable to believe her eyes. In the middle of the lawn was an ostrich.

Instinctively she turned to the phone. The ostrich must have escaped from Alex's sanctuary! Then she remembered that she had tried in vain again and again to get Alex and there was no reply.

At that moment, the dogs got out through

the back door and went racing round the garden barking at the ostrich, who looked up at them, then got aggressive, racing towards them, beak ready, long neck outstretched, running through Jon's precious plants, trampling on everything.

'Rex, come here! Sandy! Jock!' Jon screamed and screamed and finally got the dogs inside and shut them on the stoep. She went back to the phone just as the bell shrilled—her party call, three short and one long.

It was Madeleine. She sounded furious. 'Jon, is Alex there? We've been trying and trying to get him, but there's no reply.'

'I tried and there was no reply. No, he isn't here. I don't know where he is, but I must find him. His ostrich is in our garden.'

'Oh no, Jon! Wait until you hear this. The giraffes are in ours and Dad is furious. They're eating all our trees and the kids are having a whale of a time. What can have happened?'

'I haven't a clue. Maybe someone left the gates open.'

'Or knocked down the wire fence.' Madeleine gave a cry of delight. 'I bet you it was that Tim Dean!'

'Tim Dean?' Jon drew a deep breath. 'That's absurd. Why would he do a thing like that?'

'Because he hates Alex—he knows we're both in love with him. Did he propose to you?

Tim, I mean.'

'Why? I mean, why are you asking me?'

Madeleine laughed, an ugly, malicious laugh. 'Because he proposed to me three weeks ago. Yes, he did. I turned him down, of course. I told him about Alex and me.'

'About Alex and you?' Jon said dully.

'Yes, don't tell anyone, but we're secretly marrying in two weeks' time, Jon. We're not telling anyone as Alex loathes publicity and he's so wealthy the reporters would rush at him like madmen. I wouldn't mind, but what he wants goes. I told Tim I loved Alex. Did you tell him the same?'

Jon clutched the receiver. Her head was whirling, everything was happening too fast. 'I told him I couldn't marry him because I didn't love him.'

'There you are, see!' Madeleine sounded triumphant. 'I bet that made him mad. Two rich girls and both in love with a semi-millionaire. Dirty trick, isn't it, when all Tim is after is money. Have you got the police on his trail?'

'The police?'

Madeleine laughed. 'Come off it, Jon. Everyone knows he's been cheating you right, left and centre. Didn't the bank manager ring you earlier today to tell you about that enormous cheque and that Tim had forged your signature?'

Jon stifled a groan and rested her head on

her hand. That was the worst of these party-telephone lines. There was always someone like Madeleine who liked to listen in and later gossip.

'You really were fooled, weren't you, Jon?' Madeleine was gloating, now. 'Or did you do it on purpose to get yourself in a mess and then weep at Alex's feet? If you did, I wouldn't advise you to try it. If there's one species of females Alex despises, it's women who weep and use tears as weapons. It'll get you nowhere, Jon. Your best plan is to quietly sell the farm to Alex and slip away, otherwise you're going to be laughed at wherever you go, and *if*—mind, I only said if—Tim has broken down the wire fence of Alex's sanctuary and lost his valuable animals, Alex will never ever forgive you. You know that, don't you?'

Her nasty voice went on and on. Jon was hardly listening and automatically put the receiver back on the hook, not caring what Madeleine thought, but knowing she had told the truth.

If anything had happened to Alex's animals and they got hurt he would never forgive her. It was all her fault. Right from the beginning she had been a nuisance to him—and since she engaged Tim, an even worse one, it seemed. And the money she must have lost. Uncle Ned's money . . .

She went to look out of the window. The ostrich was peacefully eating in the vegetable garden, but how could she catch her and get her back in the sanctuary? If only she could contact Alex! He ought to know before too many escaped.

The phone bell rang at that moment and Jon dashed to answer it. She was breathless as she spoke:

'Jon Hampton speaking.'

'Jon, Alex here. I was wondering . . .' Alex began, but she gave him no time to finish.

'Alex! Oh, Alex, I've been trying to get you. Something awful has happened!' Her voice rose almost hysterically.

'Calm down. It can't be as bad as that. What's happened?'

'Alex, I just don't know how to tell you, but . . . but your sanctuary . . .'

'My sanctuary? What about my sanctuary?' His voice had changed, was sharp, alert. 'Now tell me calmly, don't get hysterical, because it won't help either of us.'

'Alex—your ostrich is in my garden!'

'*What?*' Alex's voice rose this time.

'And . . . and the two giraffes are at Madeleine's.'

'Oh no! What happened, Jon?' he asked. 'Any idea?'

'No, no idea at all,' she said. After all, Madeleine didn't *know* if it was Tim's doing, she only guessed it.

'Well, look, Jon, keep calm. Get your car— the ostrich won't get aggressive if you keep away from her. Drive up to the Sanctuary and see if someone left the gates open or what the guard has to say. I'm at Mbona and I'll drive back immediately. Should take about forty minutes. Maybe I should get help . . . anyhow, I'll work that out. If the wire fence has been damaged by a poacher, see if you can get it fixed to stop any more escapes. See you!' Then there was the click as he hung up.

Jon sat back, a wave of relief flooding through her. That was it! Why hadn't she thought of that? Of course it was a poacher. How could they have imagined Tim . . .'

Yet Tim had done other, equally wrong things. Forgery, theft, goodness knows what else. She hadn't mentioned it to Alex as she felt it was of less importance than his sanctuary. That had priority.

Leaving the dogs shut in, she went out quietly, got into her car and drove away, the ostrich completely ignoring her.

She drove up the winding rough track and saw, before she reached them, that both gates were intact and closed. She was glad that the African, sitting in his sentry-box half asleep, was Horace, for he spoke reasonably good English and she was able to make herself understood.

His face was horrified. 'The ostrich and jaafs? Oh, missis, that is bad. What will the master say?'

'He wants us to go round the fence and see

if we can find an opening. Better get in my car.'

'Yes, missis.' Carefully he came through the gates and locked them behind him.

There was quite a wide but corrugated path on the outside of the tall wire fence, but it took them twenty minutes before they found the opening. The wire had been cut down in a straight line and bent back, leaving quite a large opening. The awful part for Jon was that it was where the wire fence divided her land and Alex's!

Together, she and Horace forced the wire to join and tied it up with a bit of string Horace luckily had in his pocket. It was only a temporary remedy, but Horace told her he would get help and do it with wire.

'The master will be angry, very angry,' he said sadly.

As she drove him back to the entrance, Jon wondered how many of the animals had escaped. Alex had some beautiful birds, tall graceful cranes with their long thin legs, some lovely flamingoes with that wonderful pink colouring, many peacocks, even some penguins who had their own pool. Apart from them, there were other animals, the impala, the two buffaloes, and goodness knew what else. It was going to be a terrible job to get them all back safely.

As she drove round and the entrance gates came in sight, she saw Alex roaring up the hill in his car. He must be upset, for he didn't usually travel at that rate.

He was waiting by the gates as she drove up. 'Well?'

'We've found where the wire was cut and tied it up temporarily. Horace said he'd get help and take wire along.'

'I'd better go along and look. Heard of any more animals escaped?'

'No. Maybe people will phone. Would you like me to sit at your phone and take messages?'

Alex frowned. 'No, I can manage, thanks. By the way, where was the wire cut?'

Jon swallowed nervously. 'On . . . where . . . where your land and mine meet.'

'That's odd. I wouldn't think a poacher would do it that side. The other is wild country. Anyhow, thanks for the help, Jon. Come on with me, Horace. The sooner we get that fence fixed the better.'

'Alex, what shall I do about the ostrich?' Jon asked, feeling a little snubbed, for she only wanted to help.

'Just ignore her. She's a greedy creature and will probably come back when it's her meal time,' he said, and started his engine and drove away.

Jon drove back slowly, thinking hard. Somehow she didn't want to go home. She didn't want the phone to ring and perhaps Madeleine's malicious voice be there, asking questions, constantly telling her how much Alex loved her. Could it be true about the secret wedding? Somehow she had a feeling that it wasn't. The way Alex had spoken of Madeleine, though he was sorry for her, had not been loving.

She drove slowly and wondered if she did know how Alex behaved when he loved someone. After all, she had believed he was in love with her mother.

What was she to do? She knew one thing; Alex would never forgive her for the trouble she had caused. His years of hard work, his beloved sanctuary damaged, plus Tim's thefts and lies and forgery. How Alex would despise her, what a splendid chance it would give him to cut her down to size. She could just imagine him saying:

'Well, little Jon, a fine mess you have made of things, haven't you? It's a blessing your poor Uncle Ned isn't here to see it. He'd be really disappointed.'

That was it. Uncle Ned had put his beloved Jabula in her hands and she had failed to look after it. What could she do?

She knew one thing. She didn't want to go on living here, knowing everyone was laughing, that they were talking about her, nudging each other when she entered the store. No, she couldn't bear that.

Suddenly she knew one man who could help her—old Cliff! She began to drive faster. He lived alone in a small stone cottage close to the little church. Would he be home now? She had no idea of the time. Glancing at her watch, she was startled to see it was just lunch time. So much had happened that morning she had felt sure it was much later. Maybe old Cliff would be home then. At least she could try. She couldn't phone him, for there were often listeners on the party line.

She easily found the small stone cottage and parked alongside Cliff's dusty truck. At the same moment, Cliff came to stand in the doorway, in his grubby shorts and open shirt. He held a chicken leg in his hand. 'My, this is an honour,' he joked. 'Come and have a bite.'

It was cool inside and she helped herself to a piece of cold chicken and accepted an ice-cold drink. Now she was there, she wasn't sure what she wanted to ask him. He waited patiently, talking about the weather, such dramatic changes, and the latest news in the paper as if he sensed her difficulty in finding the right words. After they had eaten, his houseboy brought in two cups of coffee and they sat in the open doorway.

'Well?' he asked gently.

Jon leaned forward. 'Cliff, I . . . is it true they're going to build a dam in our valley?'

His beetling eyebrows nearly met. 'The dam? They've talked of it for the past ten years and are likely to talk of it for another ten. Why?'

She looked at her hands, stretching her fingers.

'I was told that . . . that they'd pay very good compensation.'

Cliff gave a snort. 'Whoever told you that was talking through his hat. Compensation never equals—or very rarely—the normal price you'd get if you sell it, but no one is going to give you a good price while there's the danger of the dam hanging over their heads.'

Puzzled, she stared at him. 'But, Cliff, would the compensation have been more than what Alex offered Uncle Ned for the farm?'

Cliff spluttered as he drank his coffee. 'Good grief, no! Alex is crazy at times, but he loved your Uncle Ned. He knew the old man wanted the money to leave to his little heir, so Alex offers the old man a ridiculously high sum. Maybe that was why Ned refused it. He hated charity.'

'But he was quite well off.'

'Who? Old Ned? Once upon a time he was, but not in the past years. He was always saving money and sending it overseas to some relation . . .' He paused as he saw the horror on Jon's face. 'Have I said the wrong thing?'

'No, but . . . but we were the relations. I didn't know until Alex told me that my mother and I had been living on Uncle Ned's money all these years.'

'He was a fine old chap, but crafty. When he had an idea he pursued it and thought up

252

some amazing ways of cheating fate.' Cliff chuckled and yawned. 'Afraid I've got to get started, Jon. Anything else you want to know?'

She hesitated, looked round the small room that led on to the front door. It was dark and cool but furnished with simplicity—a typical single man's home.

'Tell you one thing, little Jon,' Cliff said slowly. 'If you're in trouble, go to Alex. He's a fine guy. He wanted to buy the farm from you before you knew of the dam and he'd have given you double what it's worth. How many men, even when they're rich, would do that? He's one you can trust.'

'Yes, I know,' Jon said sadly.

She drove home and went into the empty house. The ostrich had gone. The dogs were racing about madly but came to welcome her. Inside, she got herself a cold drink and sat down on the stoep. She looked at the mountains sadly. Soon they would no longer be there—or rather, she would no longer be where she was. She had made up her mind. It was the only solution.

She saw the *induna* walking by and hurried out to him. Quickly she asked him about the staff.

'Have any left lately? Why do they go to work for Mr Roe?'

The *induna* smiled. 'Mr Roe is a good boss. Mr Dean bad.'

'Well, Mr Dean has gone. How was he bad?'

The *induna* scratched his head and looked at the sky, then at her. He was a tall, dark-skinned man in loose khaki trousers and a gay red and white shirt. 'Well, Mr Dean lie and cheat and lose his temper. Mr Roe, he's tough but keeps his word. That's why they go. Now they come back to work for you,' he promised, with a big smile.

'Thank you,' she said, and turned. She hadn't been able to tell him that she wouldn't be there.

She wondered who would buy the farm, if they would love it as much as she did and as Uncle Ned had.

Alex came to see her after tea. She had sensed that he would, though she didn't know why. She had showered and changed into her favourite kaftan and was sitting on the stoep, hands folded meekly, as she watched him get out of his car and walk towards her.

'Well?' she said as he came up the steps and then sat down opposite her. She was filled with a strange feeling of serenity. She had made her decision. It would not be easy to carry out, but at least it made her know where she was going. No more drifting for her. She would go away as far as she could just as soon as she could.

'Most of the animals are back,' Alex told her. 'Luckily whoever did the job had little knowledge of the sanctuary. Where he cut the wire, few animals go. There's some sort of weed there they don't like.'

254

'Was it difficult to get the giraffes back?'

'It wasn't easy, but I got help.' Alex sat back and folded his arms. 'What's this gossip I hear about Tim Dean?'

She clasped her hands tightly. 'It isn't gossip. It's the truth.' Quickly she told him of the bank manager's phone call, of her finding Tim's clothes gone, plus the radio and the clock they had lent him.

'Actually they were Mum's, which makes it worse.'

'Is it true he forged your signature?'

Alex's voice was calm, almost kind. Very different from what she had expected.

'Yes, he must have done. I would never have signed a cheque that size without asking what it was for.'

'Well, the police are after him. It seems he makes this his way of living—finding a lone woman with a farm and cheating her. He's done it before and been in jail.'

'Tim has?' Jon was startled. 'I'm not very good at judging character,' she added sadly.

'We all of us have to learn,' Alex said, almost comfortingly.

She looked at him and knew that if she did not take the final step soon she would never take it.

'Alex,' she said slowly, 'I'm going to sell Jabula.'

His head jerked up and she saw amazement in his eyes.

'Why?'

'You know why.' Her voice was unsteady, so she gave herself a moment to recover and then went on, 'I've made a horrible mess of everything. I've wasted Uncle Ned's carefully saved money, engaged a criminal as a manager, I'm even half sure it was he who cut the wire of the sanctuary,' she added bravely. I'm afraid I'm no good as a farmer. No good at . . . at all.'

'You could learn in time. We could find you a good manager.'

She leaned forward, her face earnest. 'But that isn't the same, Alex. It's no longer *your* own farm. It's . . . it's like buying frozen pastry to make a chicken pie—you never feel it's *your* pie, somehow.'

'Who will you sell it to?' he asked, almost casually.

She stared at him. This was the time for the truth.

'I'd like to sell it to you, Alex, but I can't. You remember that letter from Uncle Ned you gave me? The one Mum couldn't see and that you said you could see, but I tore it up?'

'I remember,' he said coldly. She shivered for a moment.

'Well, Uncle Ned said . . . I've never been able to understand why . . . he said I could trust you but I must never *sell* the farm to you. I can't think why, Alex,' she added despairingly.

She waited for him to explode, to say things about his so-called friend. Instead he smiled.

'I'm beginning to understand,' he said slowly. 'I've always said he was a crafty old devil.'

Suddenly she was crying—not hysterical sobs, but the tears just slid down her cheeks and she couldn't stop them.

'He was a wonderful man,' she said.

And then Alex was on his knees by her side, his arms round her. She rested her head on his shoulder and let the tears come. It was as if they had been bottled up inside her for so long that they could not wait to slide down her wet cheeks. Somehow, she didn't know why, but it seemed the most natural thing in the world to be in Alex's arms, to weep on his shoulder, to feel his hand gently stroking her hair.

And then she realized he was talking. And the things he said were so amazing that she could not believe them, and yet she knew from the way he was speaking that he meant every word of them.

'Darling Jon,' he was saying, 'I love you so much. When we're married, you can give me Jabula as a wedding present. That was what Uncle Ned wanted. He was always talking to me of how lovely you were, what a wonderful wife you would be, how I would love you.'

Jon lifted her head, the tears had stopped. 'You knew I was a girl?' she said slowly, remembering that day at the airport.

'Of course I did. But I was the only one Uncle Ned told. I knew, too, that he wanted us to marry. He's always been the greatest matchmaker, but I didn't think he'd succeed this time. I'm wary about marriage, as you know, Jon darling, and I thought that no girl could rival my work. And then I saw you.'

She moved a little way away, but his arms tightened. Their faces were close.

'Why did you tease me that day? Pretend you thought I was a boy?'

'Because you looked so sad, darling and because I fell in love with you the moment I saw you and I had to do something to make you see me.'

'See you?'

He brushed her hair back and dried her tears.

'Yes, love, see me. I'm just a man, twelve years older than you. I wanted to make you *see* me.'

A little smile curved her mouth. 'You succeeded. I hated you!'

Alex laughed as if delighted. 'Don't you see that was why your uncle said you mustn't sell the farm to me? He wanted to make you wonder why. He wanted to make you see me as an individual, someone a little mysterious, perhaps frightening. And it worked, bless him. It worked!'

He caught her close and kissed her, not roughly as he had done before but first gently and then more firmly. She linked her arms round his neck and let the wonder of the touch of his lips go through her.

Over his shoulders, she saw the golden sun as it shone on the mountains before it began to set. Her beautiful blue mountains.

'Oh, Uncle Ned darling,' she whispered, 'how can I ever thank you enough?'